LIFE'S A FUNNY PROPOSITION, HORATIO

After his father's death two years ago, Horatio and his mother moved to a small town to live with his grandfather, O.P. Horatio has new friends and a Siberian Husky, Silver Chief, but even they can't help him when his mom starts dating again. Then, worst of all, O.P.'s beloved dog Millie runs away and doesn't come back. Horatio has already lost someone who meant the world to him. How many more losses will he have to bear?

"Effervescing with humor, sprinkled with apt Shakespearian quotations and sweetened with a hint of first romance, this little book packs quite a wallop."

—*Publishers Weekly*

"Capable of bringing tears but not wallowing in them, this is a matter-of-fact book that leaves Horatio (and the reader) with a realistic mixture of sadness for losses past and pleasure in the daily gains of growing up."

—*Bulletin of the Center for Children's Books*

"Polikoff has carefully crafted a story that focuses on changes, personal growth, and relationships that build bridges among people of all ages and stages."

—*School Library Journal*, starred review

Life's
a Funny Proposition,
Horatio

Barbara Garland Polikoff

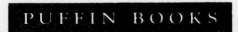
PUFFIN BOOKS

PUFFIN BOOKS
Published by the Penguin Group
Penguin Books USA Inc., 375 Hudson Street, New York, New York 10014, U.S.A.
Penguin Books Ltd, 27 Wrights Lane, London W8 5TZ, England
Penguin Books Australia Ltd, Ringwood, Victoria, Australia
Penguin Books Canada Ltd, 10 Alcorn Avenue, Toronto, Ontario, Canada M4V 3B2
Penguin Books (N.Z.) Ltd, 182–190 Wairau Road, Auckland 10, New Zealand

Penguin Books Ltd, Registered Offices: Harmondsworth, Middlesex, England

First published in the United States of America by Henry Holt and Company, Inc., 1992
Reprinted by arrangement with Henry Holt and Company, Inc.
Published in Puffin Books, 1994

3 5 7 9 10 8 6 4 2

LIBRARY OF CONGRESS CATALOGING-IN-PUBLICATION DATA
Polikoff, Barbara Garland.
Life's a funny proposition, Horatio/Barbara Garland Polikoff.
p.   cm.
"First published in the United States of America by Henry Holt . . .
1992"—T.p. verso.
Summary: Horatio finds life a strange experience as he tries to
cope with the death of his father, his mother's new boyfriend, and
having to give up his room to his grandfather.
"Ages 10 and up"—P. [4] of cover.
ISBN 0-14-036644-X
[1. Death—Fiction.   2. Grief—Fiction.   3. Grandfathers—Fiction.
4. Conduct of life—Fiction.]   I. Title.
PZ7.P75284Li   1994   [Fic]—dc20   93-36238   CIP   AC

Printed in the United States of America

For my friend Becky Glass

Life's

a Funny Proposition,

Horatio

1

I t was snowing too hard to go ice skating on the lake, so Horatio was just hanging around. "Driving her up the wall" was the way his mom put it. So she kept suggesting things for him to do. Exciting things like writing a thank-you note to his Aunt Bella for the slime green bathrobe she had given him for his birthday. Or taking his clothes off his bookshelves and putting them in drawers. Or using cleaning fluid on the rug where he had spilled taco sauce.

What he really wanted to do was to play some of his new tapes loud enough to blast the icicles off the roof. No way. Now that O.P. (his grandfather, the Old Professor) had come to live with them, he had to keep his music low or listen through headphones. O.P. was always working on his book and needed quiet.

Then his mom had come up with one of her "creative" ideas. "Write a list of things you really believe." She was big on self-expression. His, not hers. Anyhow, she promised to make pecan pancakes for him while he was writing his list. Anything for pecan pancakes.

He went to his room, kicked stuff into corners to clear a space on the floor, put on a tape (pretty low), laid out a sheet of brown wrapping paper and with a fat purple marker began to write:

Horatio Tuckerman's List of Absolute Truths

1. Being a kid is the pits.
2. Cigarettes should be banned from the earth just like poison gas.
3. When someone dies, the hardest thing to get used to is that they just aren't around anymore.
4. Boring people who have low, mumbling voices shouldn't be allowed to be schoolteachers. They should be dentists, because when someone is yanking your tooth out you don't hear what they're saying anyhow.
5. Silver Chief is the best dog in the world.

He put the one in about dentists because that's what his mom was and he was feeling subversive. (Another of his mom's ideas was to keep a record of new words. *Subversive* was the first one on his list.) He would rather she did something more motherish—teaching kindergarten or writing cookbooks like Erik and Angie's mom. Having a mom who was a dentist was just one more thing that made him different from other kids. There were enough things already.

To begin with, there was his name. How could a parent who loved a baby name him Horatio? Well, his father, Joshua Tuckerman (the Young Professor), had.

He had written plays and taught Shakespeare at a university. His favorite play was *Hamlet,* and one of his favorite characters was—you guessed it—Hamlet's friend, Horatio.

Which brought Horatio back to Absolute Truth #1. Being a kid is the pits. The reason: you have no rights. Your father likes Shakespeare and so you end up with a weird name. He had thought of dropping Horatio and just using his initials, H.T., but his dad had said for sure some clown was going to call him Hot Turds.

Now that his dad was dead, being mad at him for picking the name Horatio didn't feel right. If he was going to be mad about anything, it would be because his dad had smoked. He had finally quit by going to a hypnotist, but by then he had already smoked two packs a day for twenty years. Horatio had seen a photograph in the doctor's office of what a smoker's lungs looked like. Black, like burnt spareribs. The guy who didn't smoke had lungs clean and pink as bubble gum.

Sometimes when Horatio was in bed at night, his mind would flash to his father. There'd be this window in his dad's chest and through it he'd see these scary black lungs. Your mind does terrible things to you, mostly when you're feeling bad already. As if it's your enemy and wants to make you suffer.

More on names. His was Tuckerman and his mom's was Berg because she had kept her own name when she married. When they had moved to Wisconsin after his father died, his teachers, his friends' parents, anyone who had met him before they had met his mom would call her Mrs. Tuckerman or Dr. Tuckerman. She'd tell them her name was Berg, and they'd look at her as if she'd pulled up her sleeve and showed them a tattoo.

Still more on names. When Myron the Moron and Kevin the Creep found out he was a vegetarian, they started calling him Turnip instead of Tuckerman. They thought that was cosmically funny. They probably thought it was funny to lock lambs up in tiny sheds so they couldn't move! That makes the lambs' meat tender. Sick! When he had first read about that—bizang!—no more lamb chops on his plate! And then when that cow at the County Fair looked at him with her big brown eyes and he thought, Hey, Elsie, a hunk of you might end up on my hamburger bun, that was it for hamburgers. His Aunt Bella had once served a cow's tongue, curling pink and pimply on a big blue plate. He had nearly thrown up.

But the most important difference between him and other kids was, and always would be, that his father had died. He knew kids who didn't live with their fathers because their parents were divorced, but they all had them. And they could be with them, even if it was just on weekends. No one else's dad had died of lung cancer.

Folding the list like a newspaper, he went into the kitchen to deliver it, hoping to see his mom stacking pancakes on the griddle. No mom. More importantly, no pancakes. The only thing on the stove was a pot of coffee. Then he heard her laugh coming from her bedroom. She was talking on the phone. Probably to Sue Ellen. Ever since his dad had died, she talked to Sue Ellen a lot. He wished Sue Ellen lived close by. She and his mom had gone to college together and they always

4

had a lot to say to each other. Sue Ellen could really make his mom laugh.

The coffee smelled good. Like chocolate. He poured a little into a cup and took a sip. Bitter! Once, after his dad had tasted one of his mom's new coffees, he had groaned and said, "Evie, this tastes like mud! It must have been ground this morning." His mom acted as if she didn't think that was funny, but she couldn't help smiling.

Horatio underlined the words *absolute truths* three times, then taped the list to his mom's closed door, making enough noise to let her know he was doing it.

"Evie!"

O.P. was calling his mom. His voice sounded funny. Geez, he'd hate being old. Having a metal box inside you to keep your heart ticking.

"Evie!"

Horatio hurried to O.P.'s room (which had been his room three months ago). O.P. was sitting on the floor, breathing hard.

"Help me up, Horatio, please."

Horatio bent down and grabbed O.P. around the shoulders. The old man's cold hands gripped his as he lifted him into a chair. O.P. was light as a potato chip. It was scary he was so light.

"Grandpa, are you all right?"

"My glasses fell under the bed. I bent down to get them and couldn't stand up."

"I'll get Mom."

"No, I'm fine. A-one."

"She's been talking an hour already. I'll get her."

"Just call Mollie in, Horatio. She's too old to be out in this freezing weather."

Horatio hadn't known O.P.'s dog, Mollie, was outside. He went into the kitchen and opened the door. A gust of wind slapped him and he stepped back. It was cold! Snow covered everything. A drift, white and smooth as meringue on a lemon pie, had built up against the garage and the frosted branches of the willow were really weeping now. As he looked out across the snowy yard to the lake it was hard to tell where the shore ended and the water began.

Silver Chief was sleeping in a curled ball under the oak tree, snow dusting his fur. But where was Mollie?

Horatio drew a deep breath and yelled, "Mollie!" Snow stung his eyes and he squinted, scanning the neighbors' yards and the shoreline for a large, shaggy black dog. He wanted to see Mollie so badly that for a second he thought he did see her.

"Mollie!" he hollered, fighting the wind. *"Mollie!"*

2

When someone dies, they just aren't around anymore. You don't see them walking dripping wet out of the shower looking for a dry towel. Or pouring coffee into a Mickey Mouse mug and sitting with you while you eat your granola. You don't hear their computer clicking away behind the closed door of their room, or their laugh bursting out when you tell them something funny. You don't see their glasses lying in places they didn't know they left them. And then when you returned them, wow, the thanks you'd get, as if you'd really done something wonderful.

The Young Professor had five pairs of reading glasses, all bought at Walgreens. When he was writing a play, which was most of the time, he'd throw the door of his study open, look around like a wild man, drop his glasses on the kitchen table, in a plant, on the refrigerator, and rush out to Lincoln Park and walk along the lake until he was calm enough to come back in the house. And then the question, "Has anyone seen my glasses?"

The answer would always be no. He'd begin yanking up couch cushions, crawling under his desk, lifting up books. If he didn't find the glasses in five minutes flat, he'd run out to Walgreens and buy a new pair.

One crazy day, four pairs of glasses turned up at once. If Horatio had been his father, he would have been disgusted with himself. But not his dad. He had lined them up on his desk and smiled as if it were a big accomplishment to have four pairs of brown-rimmed glasses from Walgreens, priced $9.99.

Horatio had found a pair of those glasses in between the couch cushions a month after his dad had died. He had wanted to yell, "Hey, Dad, guess what I found?" But he couldn't. His dad just wasn't there and never would be, swiveling around on his chair and smiling, wearing that ragged Peanuts sweatshirt with the faded words HOW CAN WE LOSE WHEN WE'RE SO SINCERE?

It was at times like that when he really knew what it meant to have someone die. When you wanted them right there in front of you so bad that you felt sick. The kind of sick that pulls all your guts down into your stomach and won't let go of them, until maybe the next day when you go to chess club and get involved in a dynamite game.

He didn't tell his mom he had found the glasses. He just put them in his bottom drawer, stuffed behind the old Peanuts sweatshirt. He had asked her if he could have that sweatshirt when she was packing his father's clothes to give away. She had held the sweatshirt against her cheek.

"I can still feel him in it," she said, and then handed it

to him. Her face was stony. No expression. It seemed as if she had made herself numb so she could get through the packing. He felt so bad for her. He wanted to hug her and try to make her feel better, but he was afraid he'd cry.

She hadn't been stony at the funeral, though. He knew because he looked at her a lot and most of the time she was crying. He hadn't known where else to look. He hated people staring at him, feeling sorry for him when he didn't even know who they were.

His dad had asked to be cremated, so there wasn't any coffin at the funeral. His mom explained that the ashes go in a box and the box goes into a vault in a cemetery unless you want the ashes scattered somewhere. His Uncle Stewart, O.P., and his mom had buried his dad's ashes in the park by the Shakespeare statue that his dad had liked so much. When Horatio was little, his dad would lift him up and sit him between Shakespeare's pointed shoes. It was fun being up there, and he'd grab onto the big bow on one of the shoes and not let go when his dad wanted to take him down.

His tenth birthday was just five days after his dad had died, and Uncle Stewart took him on a weekend backpack in the Wisconsin woods. At night they made a campfire, and when it was time to go to sleep, Uncle Stewart had stirred the ashes, spreading them so they wouldn't ignite again. Horatio got so sick seeing the ashes that he had to run into the trees and vomit.

Uncle Stewart was a dentist too. Weird, two people in the same family wanting to poke around in a lot of mucky

9

mouths. It was Stewart's idea that Horatio and his mom move to Spring Creek and that she be his partner in his dental office.

After that he and his mom talked a lot about going to Wisconsin. She said she knew he'd love living in the country, and she was right. Too many people in Chicago, too many buildings, too many cars.

He had always loved Spring Creek. There were woods and lakes and raspberries growing along the back roads, and if you got to them before the birds did, they were sweet and juicy. In the morning if he took a walk with his mom and Uncle Stewart, they might see a deer feeding. It would look at them, its face so alert with its licorice nose and big, soft eyes, and then it would run off, its white tail the last thing he would see as the deer vanished into the woods.

His mom wasn't much of a city person either. Besides being a dentist she was a potter, and her dream was to have a studio big enough for a giant kiln. In Chicago she had to rent a studio in a crummy neighborhood where she was afraid of being mugged.

So he hadn't really been surprised when she sat on his bed one Sunday morning and told him that she had finally decided that they should move to Spring Creek. She had talked real fast.

"I hope it's okay with you, Horatio. I know you don't want to leave your friends. It'll be hard at first, but you'll make new ones. And Stewart found a good house for us on Moccasin Lake. It's a real country house, one story made out of cedar, with a full basement for a studio and . . ." She had stopped, and a smile had crept onto

10

her face. He had noticed it because she didn't smile that much since his dad had died.

" . . . it has a big, fenced-in yard, perfect for a dog." Her smile got even bigger and she handed him a white card printed with the words *Tamika Borland, Siberian Huskies, 777 Half-Day Road, Schaller, Wisconsin.*

He had jumped up as if he had dynamite in his jeans and hugged her. "Mom, I want a male, and his name will be . . ."

"Silver Chief!" she said, hugging him back. "Dog of the North!"

And then they both laughed, and he had run and taped the white card in the middle of his dresser mirror so that if he stood a certain way, the words *Siberian Huskies* were written across his forehead. While his mom telephoned Uncle Stewart, he looked through some books on his closet floor until he found his copy of *Silver Chief, Dog of the North.* His dad had given him the book for his ninth birthday. It had been his dad's favorite when he was a boy, and Horatio loved it too. He propped pillows under his head, stretched out on his bed and opened the book to Chapter One. He could almost recite the first sentences by memory.

Across the brooding desolation of the frozen Northlands drifted the eerie, mournful howl of wolves. It died away and a heavy silence closed in upon the stark land. . . .

3

oratio shivered as the wind slammed the kitchen door behind him.

O.P. looked at him anxiously. "No luck, Horatio?"

"Mollie must have gone farther than she meant to, Grandpa, and it's taking her a while to get back."

"Is Silver Chief in his house?"

"No, he'd rather be outside. He loves the snow."

A shadow of a smile crossed O.P.'s face. "It's his feather bed."

"I'm going to look for Mollie. I'll be right back."

"Your mother might not like that, Horatio. It's getting dark. You'd better ask her."

"She's still on the phone. She won't care."

"Well, don't stay out too long."

Silver Chief rose and stretched when he saw Horatio. His fur glistened with snow, and his blue eyes were the color of the lake in summer.

12

"Come on, Silver Chief, let's find Mollie."

Silver Chief's ears stood up like small flags that signaled, "All systems go."

Mollie often explored the beach, so Horatio walked across the frozen sand to the lake. It was tough going because his boots punched through the icy crust to the soft snow underneath. It was like pulling his feet out of a hole with each step.

Silver Chief ran along the shoreline so swiftly that his paws hardly made a mark. Horatio could see no other prints. Mollie must not have come this way, unless falling snow had already covered her tracks. Across the lake a dog darted out of some trees, and his heart leaped. Mollie?

He stared. It wasn't Mollie. Too fat and too big. Mollie was thin and kind of bony, like O.P.

Nobody else in the world was outdoors. That's the way it seemed, anyway. The ice fishermen's blue and red tents were empty. The fish were probably swimming so deep they'd never come up for bait.

He put his hands on either side of his mouth and yelled, "Mollie!" so loudly his throat ached.

If only she'd suddenly appear!

His mom was waiting in the kitchen when he returned. She looked at him expectantly, her face clouding with worry when he shook his head.

"But Mollie never stays out this long, Horatio. Could she have gotten lost?"

"She probably doesn't feel like coming back inside yet. She likes the snow."

"Well, you'd better go tell O.P. He's in the living room."

"You tell him."

His mom wrapped her arms around her chest as if she were cold. "If anything's happened to Mollie . . ." She sighed and walked out of the kitchen.

So where were his pecan pancakes? You'd think she would have had them waiting hot on the griddle.

He swung open the refrigerator door and peered inside. Two cartons of plain yogurt, a carton of coffee yogurt, cranberry juice, mushrooms, tofu swimming in water, two foil packets of leftover fish, two packages of pita bread and some dead-looking lettuce. Nothing good. He shut the door. He needed something hot.

His mom had been forgetting a lot of things that she was going to do for him since O.P. had come to live with them three months ago. O.P. had suffered a heart attack, and the doctor said he shouldn't live alone. That's when Horatio's mom got the idea that O.P. should come to Spring Creek. She thought it would be good if Horatio had the company of a man in the house. But it wasn't as if he and O.P. really knew each other. O.P. had lived in London and taught Shakespeare at a university there. He'd just visit them for two weeks in the summer, and then Horatio's dad would go to London during the winter vacation to see him. The airplane fare was too expensive for them all to go.

O.P. had a white beard and hair that was wild because he would comb his hands through it when he was reading. His hair had been black, like Horatio's and his dad's. Black hair and nearsighted brown eyes ran in

14

his dad's family. Plus being tall and thin. His dad had been thin, but with good muscles in his arms and legs from working out at the gym. O.P. was thin, zero. He was a real bookworm. Who ever heard of a worm having muscles?

Horatio planned to work out too and carry sixty pounds in his backpack like his dad, clear up Mount Rainier without losing a breath. But no brown-rimmed glasses for him. He had convinced his mom to let him wear contacts when they had moved to Spring Creek.

Well, he wasn't going to ask for those pancakes. Forget it. He'd starve.

He opened the kitchen door, bracing himself for a slap from the wind, and yelled for Silver Chief.

The husky came loping toward him, ran into the house and stood looking at Horatio intently, his eyes unblinking, his tail up.

"Want a biscuit, Silver Chief?" He teased Silver Chief by pretending to put the biscuit in his own mouth. Silver Chief cocked his head to one side and looked at him curiously. When he gave him the biscuit, Silver Chief carried it under the dining-room table, propped it upright between his paws and took a small bite.

"Silver Chief has better table manners than you do," his mom liked to say. "He doesn't gulp his food."

Horatio wished Erik weren't at a drum lesson so he could call him and talk to him about Mollie. This waiting was terrible, although he was telling himself he wasn't really worried. A dog's a dog. They run off sometimes, but they come back. Especially Mollie. She was so attached to O.P. She'd never run away.

15

Hey, he thought, this might be a good time to call Erik because Angie might answer the phone. Yeah, this was the perfect time to call. Why not?

I'll tell you why not, Horatio answered himself. Because you're the world's biggest nerd. You've got as much guts as tofu when it comes to girls. Angie, especially. Admit it. On a scale of one to ten on NERDINESS WITH GIRLS, you're eleven!

His mom and O.P. came into the kitchen, interrupting his conversation with himself. O.P. looked more worried than ever.

"Grandpa, Mollie'll be all right. She can take care of herself."

"You're right, Horatio." O.P. sat down at the table and opened the Sunday paper. "We should just go about our business."

"Our business should be eating," Evie said. "I made vegetable soup and there's salad and Martha's millet bread."

I knew it, Horatio thought. She forgot the pecan pancakes.

It wasn't the greatest Sunday dinner. It was actually pretty awful. They were all pretending they weren't listening for Mollie's bark at the door. When the wind blew a garbage can over, they all jumped. O.P. kept looking at his watch, and then he'd look at the kitchen clock. His mom would try to make conversation and come up with all kinds of stuff, like her mind was a drawer and she was digging out all the junk at the bottom.

"When I was driving to work, the car in front of me

was plastered with these stupid bumper stickers," she said. " 'If you don't like the way I drive, get off the sidewalk,' and 'I've lost a lot of things, but the one I miss most is my mind.' There was one I couldn't read and I kept trying to and almost got into an accident. Bumper stickers ought to be outlawed."

"You can't outlaw bumper stickers!" Horatio exploded. "That would be against freedom of speech."

"But they present a clear danger," O.P. said with a hint of a smile.

The phone rang and his mom jumped up and grabbed it. "Hello?"

Let it be someone calling to say they found Mollie, Horatio prayed.

His mom's voice went flat. "Yes, Stewart. No, that's okay. We're on a funny schedule today. Mollie went out and hasn't come back, and we're a little antsy."

A little!

"What would the police do? Oh. Well, I suppose it's worth trying."

"Stewart says we should call the police," his mom said, hanging up the phone. "They'll keep an eye out for Mollie when they're patrolling. Can't lose anything."

O.P. pushed aside his plate of soup. "It's a good idea. Nothing comes of nothing."

Horatio guessed that that was a line from Shakespeare. O.P. was always quoting from Shakespeare or some other famous poet. Once, when Horatio had won a chess match after it had been called off three times, a couple of people had shaken his hand and said, "Congratulations."

Nice and simple. But not O.P.! He said, "Well, Horatio, all's well that ends well." Weird!

O.P. put the call in to the police, and things felt a little less heavy. At least they had done something.

After they had cleaned up the kitchen, his mom said with a kind of fake cheeriness, "Why don't you and O.P. play some chess?"

"I've got some homework," Horatio lied, and went into his room and closed the door. He just couldn't be with them anymore. He needed space. He felt beat.

He looked out the window. The moon was a little more than half full. It looked blurred, as if a kid had drawn it with chalk and then smudged it by accident. Not a star anywhere.

Usually he liked the night. Nighttime said to him, "You can stop trying now, and just be a lump. And no one will know."

Lumping out, he called it. He stretched full length on the bed and pulled *Silver Chief* from under his pillow.

He had read just two pages when he heard a knock on his door. Even before he had time to say Come in, his mother walked into the room. She had taken a shower and was wearing a white bathrobe with her initials, E.B., on the pocket. She said they stood for Extra Busy. She was really good looking. Everyone said so. Erik thought she looked like the model on a TV commercial advertising stuff for sinus relief. Not that she looked like she had bad sinuses, but the model had long brown hair too, and eyes that kind of turned up, Chinese-like.

"Horatio, I'm worried about O.P. This stress is bad

18

for him. Chess might take his mind off Mollie." She motioned to the book. "It looks like you've finished your homework."

"Well, I just couldn't concentrate on chess right now."

His mom didn't understand. Her face told him that. She was mad.

"I'm not going to beg you." She closed the door pretty hard.

So now he felt crummy.

He put the book back under his pillow and walked into the dining room to see if Silver Chief was still under the table. He wasn't. His mom must have let him out. Sometimes he wished Silver Chief were more like Mollie and stayed around the house and followed him around. If O.P. was sitting on a chair on the sun porch, Mollie would lie next to him, sometimes with her face resting on his shoe. She even slept in O.P.'s bed. O.P. said he hadn't let her do that in London, but when she came to Wisconsin things were so different, he decided she needed to be close to him. Now O.P. couldn't sleep without her.

Horatio walked back into the kitchen and opened the door. The wind had died down and smoky clouds hid the moon. Across the lake he could see houses, their windows yellow squares of light. Could someone in one of those houses have seen Mollie and taken her in? But she had a name tag and they would have called. She wasn't the kind of dog anyone would just keep. She was a mutt and pretty old.

Silver Chief was sleeping under the oak tree. Horatio

19

could see his black-and-white masked face, a little like a raccoon's.

O.P. wasn't reading in the big green chair by the fireplace. He was sitting doing nothing. His hands, resting on the arms of the chair, looked like the hands of one of those models in a wax museum.

"O.P., you'd better go to bed. We'll hear Mollie when she comes," his mom said. She put her book down on the coffee table. It was one of her special books on pottery. Whenever she was nervous, she'd get one of those books and leaf slowly through the photographs. It calmed her, she said.

"No, Evie. I'm staying here."

"Well, if you need me, just call. I'm bushed."

"Maybe Mollie found some warm place and decided to sleep there for the night," Horatio said, "and she'll come back in the morning."

"Maybe, Horatio. Thank you for that nice idea. Now, you better get to sleep too."

Back in his room Horatio drew the blinds, something he never did. But tonight he needed to feel closed in, safe. The darkness outside seemed an enemy, hiding Mollie, making her scared and lost.

"Horatio."

His mom again.

"Horatio, I just remembered your pecan pancakes! Why didn't you remind me?"

Horatio shrugged.

"I'll make them for you now. Okay?"

"It's kind of late to eat."

"I guess you're right." She didn't move, as if she had

something more to say but didn't know what it was. "Well, some night this week then. Double pecans. Okay?"

"Okay."

"Good night." She closed the door.

He buried himself under the covers. He knew it was being a baby to have wanted her to give him a good-night hug and tuck his blankets close around his chin and under his feet the way she used to when he was little. His dad would always stick his head in his room and say, "Sleep well, fellow."

He closed his eyes and made himself think about the chess column he had read in the paper. The move that Black made was pretty stupid. He'd cut out the column and bring it to school tomorrow to show Erik.

He hoped tomorrow wouldn't be another day with no Mollie and no news. He burrowed deeper under the covers.

4

Horatio thought he was the first one up, but when he walked into the kitchen O.P. handed him a sheet of paper with MISSING written in large letters, followed by *Mollie, a black dog with a white left ear. Please contact Benjamin Tuckerman, 777 Oriole Lane, 555-2334.* "Would you pin this up on the Moccasin Lake bulletin board, Horatio?"

"Sure." Horatio put the note in his jeans. The phone rang, and he felt O.P.'s eyes on him as he picked up the receiver.

"Hello. Yeah, just a minute, I'll see if she's up."

O.P. sank back in the chair.

"Hey, Mom, telephone!" Horatio yelled. "Are you up?"

"Yes, thanks."

He could hear her talking. She sounded pretty cheerful. Kind of fake, if you asked him.

The whole thing with Paul Miller was fake. He still couldn't believe she would go out with a guy she had met when he came in for a checkup. Weird. She had even done gum surgery on him. He probably hadn't flossed his teeth every night. Horatio hoped that he was a terrible flosser and had tons of plaque and would have to have his two front teeth pulled and a bridge put in that squeaked when he ate.

"Horatio." His mom came into the kitchen in bare feet, holding her running shoes and a red sweatshirt. Her toenails were the same red. Dumb.

"I'll make you and O.P. some oatmeal. How about it? I've got fifteen minutes before I leave for the health club."

"No, thanks, Evie," O.P. said.

"O.P., you've got to eat."

"I'll take something later."

"I'll eat granola," Horatio said. Had his mom made another date with Pink Gums Paul? She was in a pretty good mood for someone who was supposed to be worried about a missing dog.

"O.P., I'll call the police and make sure they keep checking for Mollie. Can you concentrate on your work today? I hate to think of you counting minutes until Mollie shows up."

"Minutes. Count them by sensation and not calendar, and each moment is a day . . ."

"Who said that?" Evie asked.

"Mickey Mouse," Horatio mumbled.

O.P. didn't seem to hear either of them. "Time goes on crutches . . ."

"Shakespeare," Evie said.

O.P. took Evie's hand and patted it. "Evie, I don't want you worrying about me."

23

"If there's any news, call me."

"Horatio's putting up a notice on the Moccasin Lake bulletin board. Maybe we should also be thinking of putting an item in the newspaper."

"I'll put up a notice at the health club. Half of Spring Creek walks in and out of there. Horatio, on your way home can you pick up some chili at Sunny's? I won't be home for dinner. I'm going out to an early movie with Paul."

"I don't like Sunny's chili."

"Well, get whatever you want. Their veggie pizza is good. O.P., should Horatio get some vegetable soup for you?"

"Evie, it's my heart that's weak. Not my stomach. I'll eat pizza with Horatio."

"Would you buy a couple of cinnamon buns too, Horatio?"

Cinnamon buns, not oat bran muffins, Horatio thought glumly. She's really feeling cheerful.

The bulletin board, put up by the Spring Creek Lions Club, was set in a triangle of ground where Oriole Lane and Lake Road intersected. It was a surprisingly warm day after the bitter-cold Sunday, and the icicles around the rim of the sign were melting. Horatio opened the glass door and fit his note in between announcements of a rummage sale and beginning yoga lessons. He took a red marker out of his daypack and underlined the word *missing*.

It was going to be a slow day at school. Old Willie Shakespeare had it right. Time moved on crutches. Especially if you had to listen to Gretchen Peterson read her oral report on the Industrial Revolution. Gretchen was in the acting club and was working on her enunciation. She said each word as if her tongue were outlining it in black. He slouched in his seat and closed his eyes.

At lunch he looked for Erik in the cafeteria line. He was standing next to Susie Boyce. She was talking to him and giggling. The girls were crazy about Erik. Horatio couldn't see why dimples and eyelashes thick as a broom turned the girls on, but since when was he any good at figuring out girls? Erik was pretty shy, and the attention from the girls embarrassed him. Susie Boyce was enough to embarrass a gorilla!

Erik smiled when he saw him, then asked, "What's wrong? You look terrible."

"Mollie's lost," Horatio said. "She was out all night."

"Is Mollie your sister?" Susie asked.

Horatio ignored Susie. She was like a gnat, little and pesty. "Erik, will you help me look for Mollie after school? I want to go to Thatcher Woods, but we'll pick up Silver Chief at my house first."

"Sure. I'll meet you at the flagpole, but aren't you going to eat now?"

"I'm going outside to look around."

"If you're late to math, I'll tell Mrs. Helm your little sister is lost in the woods," Susie said.

Her mother should have stepped on her when she was born, Horatio thought. He half ran out of the building, relieved that he didn't run into anyone on hall patrol.

∎ ∎ ∎

25

After school, Erik beat Horatio to the flagpole. Five minutes later, they were at Horatio's house. Ten minutes later, they were in Thatcher Woods, Silver Chief leading the way. They walked along the main trail, struck out cross-country for a while, then connected with the trail again. Snow had turned to slush, and Horatio felt water penetrate his boots. Erik was just wearing running shoes. His feet were going to get soaked.

The slushy trail slowed them down, but it didn't bother Silver Chief. Nose to the ground, he moved ahead quickly. They tried to keep up, but when there was no sign of his white plumed tail, Horatio called and Silver Chief bounded back. He waited for them and then continued to a fork in the trail, where he turned right and headed for Arrowhead Lake.

Mollie had always loved going to the lake. She'd wait for Horatio to throw a stick far out into the water and then she'd swim to retrieve it. Not Silver Chief. He was afraid of the water. If the smallest wave slapped the sand, he'd jump back and eye the lake suspiciously.

Most of the ice in the lake had melted. The fragments that were left looked like pieces from a giant puzzle. As the water moved under them they bumped into each other, making a clicking sound.

"I've got to stop a minute, Erik. There's something in my boot," Horatio said. "Keep going. I'll catch up." Erik's shoes were squishing water, but it didn't seem to bother him. He continued along the lake, Silver Chief a few feet ahead.

Horatio was tying his lace when he heard Erik's shout.

Fear tightened his chest and he started running. As soon as he saw Erik's face he knew something terrible had happened. Erik pointed to a spot farther down the shore, where Silver Chief was standing. Next to Silver Chief, Horatio made out a black, flattened shape lying on the ground.

He could hardly breathe. He had felt like this when he had walked into the hospital on the days his dad was so bad that all he could do was just lift his hand off the blanket to say hello.

As he and Erik drew close, Silver Chief lay down next to Mollie. Mollie's paws were crossed over each other as if she were sleeping. A strand of waterweed was tangled in her tail. Her black ear lay flat on a patch of snow.

"She must have run out on the lake . . . and the ice cracked. She probably just made it to . . ." His voice broke.

Erik nodded numbly.

What should they do? What would O.P. want them to do? They couldn't bury Mollie. The ground was still frozen. They'd need something, a blanket or a sheet, to carry her in if they were to bring her home.

"Let's move her under the trees for now." Horatio stooped to lift Mollie, but Erik was able to get a better grasp and carried her to a spot that Horatio covered with evergreen branches. Mollie's head settled in an awkward position and Erik shifted it so that it rested more naturally.

Horatio ran his hand along Mollie's furry back, then stroked her head. Reaching for his daypack, he pulled out his old Chicago Bears sweatshirt and covered her. Erik anchored the ends of the sweatshirt with rocks.

But Horatio couldn't tear himself away. There was something else he had to do. He picked up a stick, the kind Mollie loved to retrieve from the lake, and laid it beside her as he would have laid a flower.

In spite of his effort to hold them back, tears filled his eyes and his sobs came hard and dry. He couldn't seem to stop crying. Erik put his arm around his shoulders and held it there tightly.

A cold wind had begun to stir the trees. The light was disappearing fast. Horatio called Silver Chief, but the husky refused to leave Mollie. He had to pull him up by his collar and force him to start walking.

When they had left the lakeshore behind and were back in the trees, Silver Chief took charge and led the way. They moved through the darkening woods as silently as wolves.

5

P. was sitting at the kitchen table, reading the newspaper.

"I forgot to stop for the veggie pizza," Horatio said.

What would he say if O.P. asked if he had any news about Mollie? If he told him the truth, he could see him turning white, his heart would stop and he'd crumple to the floor like a dropped shirt. Maybe it would be easier for O.P. not to know, to think that maybe some people liked Mollie and took her home with them.

"It doesn't matter, Horatio."

"I'm going to have a peanut-butter-and-jelly sandwich. I suppose you don't want one."

O.P. smiled. "It would be a real culinary adventure."

"So, should I make you one?"

"Yes, but go easy on the peanut butter."

Horatio made the sandwiches in slow motion, spreading the jelly until it filled each corner of the bread. He felt beat. Too much heavy feeling tires you out. Crying especially. He hated crying. He had cried so much in the months after his dad had died that he would have thought he didn't have a tear left. Funny, he hadn't been embarrassed about crying in front of Erik. With any other guy he'd have felt like a baby.

It was quiet at the table with only the two of them. Just the clicking of O.P.'s teacup on the saucer. Not that Mollie made noise, but she was There, a Living Being, following O.P. around while he made his tea, dragging her old rawhide bone across the floor and dropping it at his feet so he'd throw the gummy thing for her.

Horatio thought of calling Silver Chief into the house. Would that make O.P. feel better or worse?

O.P. said the sandwich was good, but Horatio didn't think he meant it. He felt uncomfortable being alone with the old man. He was still mad at him for taking his room, even though he knew he shouldn't be. It had its own bathroom, and old people get up to go a lot during the night. But that room was big and had great windows and all his stuff fit in there with space to spare. The room he had now was much smaller. He still had things jammed in his closet that he couldn't find any place for.

O.P. put his teacup down slowly. "Horatio. I worry that Mollie may be suffering. Perhaps she's hurt and is in pain lying alone somewhere."

Horatio pushed a half-eaten sandwich aside. "Maybe someone found her and is taking good care of her," he said, but his words sounded weak even to him.

O.P. got up from the table and put his plate in the sink.

When he emptied his teacup, he banged it against the faucet and shattered it. Horatio helped pick up the pieces. The old man's hands were shaking.

"I'm not good for much, Horatio," he said. "I can't stop worrying about Mollie. 'Pleasure is often a visitant, but pain clings cruelly to us.' "

"Grandpa . . ." Horatio's heart had begun to race. "Grandpa, there's something . . ."

O.P.'s face looked so frightened that Horatio's words died in his throat.

"What is it, Horatio?"

"Oh, nothing. I . . ."

"Something's bothering you."

"I didn't want to tell you, but . . ." Horatio tried to wet his mouth with his tongue, but it was dry as wool. "Erik and I went looking for Mollie in the woods by Arrowhead Lake. She must have run out on the lake and . . . fallen through the ice." He swallowed hard, and continued. "She must have just been able to pull herself up on the sand . . . she was lying by the edge of the water . . ."

O.P. sank into a chair. His whole body went limp inside his clothes like a puppet whose strings were suddenly cut.

Horatio put his hand on his shoulder. "Grandpa. Mollie . . . she looked all right. Kind of peaceful. I covered her."

O.P. stood up and in his hurry to get to the closet, forgot his cane. "I'm going to get her, Horatio," he said, pulling his coat off a hanger.

"Grandpa, you can't carry Mollie!" Horatio took the coat from him, but O.P. grabbed it back.

"Horatio, I can't leave her in the woods. I'll carry her in a blanket." He limped across the hall to the linen closet and pulled a light blanket from a shelf. "Just tell me where the trail starts."

"Grandpa, it's dark outside. You'll trip. It's hard walking in the woods. And Mollie's heavy. I'll go back with Erik tomorrow when it's light."

But O.P. wasn't listening. He was pulling on his coat, and his eyes looked hard and bright.

Horatio handed him his cane and put on his own jacket. O.P. rushed out of the house and stepped into a puddle on his way to the car. Horatio followed close behind. The old man's eyes burned and the wind blew his white hair wildly about his face. He looked like . . . who was it? Yes—King Lear—out on the heath . . . with the storm raging around him.

O.P. didn't seem to notice Horatio in the car beside him. He drove silently, his body rigid, his hands blue-white on the steering wheel.

He *is* like King Lear, Horatio thought. Going kind of crazy with grief. It helped him to think of O.P. like that. It helped him understand his craziness.

If only the wind would stop blowing. It battered the trees and sent dead branches skittering across the road. If his mom could see them now, she'd hit the ceiling. He didn't care. He wanted her to be upset. If she hadn't taken off with Pink Gums Paul, she would have been around to stop O.P. from doing this crazy thing.

O.P. was driving faster than he usually did. Horatio was relieved when they reached Thatcher Woods.

"Grandpa, right there; pull up near the litter barrel." Horatio opened the glove compartment and took out a flashlight. He was feeling better now, more in command. He'd be able to get Mollie back. He'd have to.

Luckily the air was still warm, above freezing anyhow. The trail was sloppy, but not dangerous. He could hear the high tree branches creak as they swayed back and forth. O.P. was a little shaky, but he was managing to move ahead all right. His cane left a trail of holes in the slush.

When they reached the lake, Horatio stopped. The rough part was just beginning. He looked at O.P. He was breathing pretty hard.

"This is the lake, Horatio?"

"Yes. We go along the shore awhile. Do you want to rest?"

"No. Let's keep going."

Arrowhead looked enormous under the dark sky. Black and cold and deep. Horatio shivered. He had read that the deepest part went down twenty-six feet. But he didn't want to think about water. Only about how he was going to lift Mollie and somehow settle her in the middle of the blanket, then carry her over his shoulder back to the car. Erik would be surprised when he told him about it. His mom . . . well, he didn't know what she'd think.

"Just a little farther," he said. A log had fallen across the trail and he helped O.P. step over it.

As they got closer Horatio had an awful thought. What if some animal had found Mollie?

No. He could see the outline of Mollie's body under the evergreen trees. Everything was as they had left it. Even the stick was still in place.

"There, Grandpa. Under those trees." Horatio's stomach felt as if it were laced up tight like a boot. He took O.P.'s arm and led him slowly to where Mollie lay.

O.P. looked at the still body under the sweatshirt. Leaning on Horatio for support, he bent down and lifted the shirt from Mollie's head. He ran his fingers slowly back and forth over her face as if he were trying to imprint its contours into his own flesh.

"Can I put her in the blanket now, Grandpa?"

O.P. nodded.

Horatio stretched the blanket out on the ground. Thrusting his arms under Mollie, he managed to lift her and set her down on the fuzzy material. Then he placed the four corners of the blanket together, twisted them and pulled Mollie up so that her weight rested against his back.

"She's not too heavy for you?" O.P. asked.

"I'm okay."

He had thought it would be awful carrying Mollie. A corpse. What an ugly word. Dead dog was better. Alive. Dead. The cycle of nature. Natural, it was all natural.

But was it? Was it natural to die of cancer? Of drowning? Was it natural when a tree died after being struck by lightning?

Too much. Just too much. All he was sure of right

then was that he was carrying Mollie over his shoulder, that O.P. was walking in back of him managing his cane and the flashlight, that the wind had died down a little and that Mollie would rest safely that night in one of her favorite places, the backseat of O.P.'s old blue Ford.

After they had returned home, O.P., looking exhausted, went to his room. Horatio opened the kitchen door and peered into the trees in the back of the yard, where he thought he detected movement. Silver Chief liked to prowl back there in the nighttime. Once, the light of the moon had caught the blue of one eye as he looked toward him, making it glare like a tiny flashlight. It had startled him, pulling him out of the safe house into the wilderness, where wolves roamed the mountains at night and a boy would do well to be safely zipped into his sleeping bag in a snug tent. But he felt a shiver of excitement also. He liked the fact that Silver Chief had that streak of wildness. It made him feel closer to the wilderness, like the Mountie Jim Thorndike in Jack O'Brien's book.

Silver Chief took his time responding to Horatio's call. When he finally ran into the house, he immediately settled under the dining-room table and rested his face on his paws.

Horatio crawled under the table and lay down next to him. Usually when he did that, Silver Chief would get up and move. But he didn't tonight.

He knows I need to be with him, Horatio thought. He could feel Silver Chief's peacefulness. How could a living thing be so quiet? He rested his head on the warm, furry body and lay very still, matching his breathing to Silver Chief's.

Breathe in, breathe out, breathe in, breathe out . . . he and Silver Chief, breathing alike.

Quiet finally came. And with it, sleep.

6

"Horatio. Wake up."

Horatio opened his eyes. His mother was bending over him. He sat up and Silver Chief licked his face.

"You fell asleep under the table with Silver Chief. You'd better put him out now and come to bed. It's late."

Groggy with sleep, Horatio walked to the kitchen and opened the door for Silver Chief. What time was it? Then he felt the pain, and he remembered. Mollie.

That's what was so awful about a person or an animal dying. While you sleep you forget, but then you wake up and remember and they die all over again.

"Did you and O.P. enjoy your veggie pizzas?" his mom asked. She was wearing a dress that he had never seen before, and she had that green stuff on her eyelids. All for a little movie.

"We didn't have pizza."

"Oh? What did you have?"

"Peanut-butter-and-jelly sandwiches."

"But what did O.P. eat?"

"A peanut-butter-and-jelly sandwich."

"Horatio. Be serious."

Horatio walked to the window and squinted. His eyes felt scratchy and his throat was dry. "Erik and I went looking in the woods for Mollie. We found her at Arrowhead Lake. She . . . the ice broke. We figured she fell through. She was lying on the shore."

"Oh, no! Oh . . . how awful!"

He couldn't turn around. He knew what his mom's face would look like. "Yeah."

"Does O.P. know?"

"I didn't want to tell him . . . I was scared what it would do to him, but he was talking about how worried he was that Mollie was hurt somewhere, that she was suffering."

When he looked at his mom, she had that stony expression. She was hanging on to those black high-heeled shoes she always yanked off the minute she walked in the house.

"I went back to the woods with him to get Mollie. She's covered up in his car now."

"How did you get Mollie to the car, Horatio?"

"I carried her over my shoulder in a blanket."

"I can't imagine O.P. walking in the woods at night."

"I tried to stop him, but I couldn't. He was kind of . . . crazy. Like . . . King Lear."

Horatio's mom looked away from him and sat down on the couch. Her eyes were teary. Somehow that made him feel better. As if her crying helped him get rid of some of the heaviness inside him.

She pulled a hankie out of her purse, wiped her eyes and nose and suddenly was all business.

"We'll have to take Mollie to the vet in the morning, Horatio. I'll do it before I go to the office. O.P. will have to decide what he wants to do with her ashes."

She walked out of the room and Horatio heard her call O.P. softly, then go into his room.

Horatio hadn't known it until O.P. was living with them, but his mom really loved the old professor. He could see how she acted with him. It was too much sometimes, the attention she paid him.

"I'm going to bed, Mom," he said when she came back into the living room.

"Horatio, thank you for all your help. It must have been awful for you, finding Mollie and then having to tell O.P. I know you loved Mollie . . ."

"Yeah, well . . . how was the movie?"

"Some good laughs. You might like it."

"I probably wouldn't."

"There's a movie coming about a bear. Wonderful scenery. Maybe we can go next weekend. O.P. might enjoy it too."

"Yeah, well . . . we'll see."

Back in his room he flopped on his bed. He was too beat to get out of his clothes, to brush his teeth, for sure to floss them. He couldn't believe that his mom flossed every single night. Did she floss the night his dad died?

Stupid! What kind of stupid things was he thinking? He yanked off his jeans and crawled under the blankets. As soon as he closed his eyes he saw Mollie breaking through the ice. He tried to think of something else, but the scene kept replaying in his mind. He sat up, switched on the light and reached for *Silver Chief, Dog of the North* and turned to the chapter in which the husky was gone so long that Jim was afraid he had returned to the wilderness forever. And then Silver Chief comes back. He loved that part. He read until his eyes closed and the book slipped out of his hands.

Erik hadn't been at school that day. Horatio was going to stop at his house, but then he thought he'd better call from school first. Maybe Angie would answer. He hoped so. She was a year younger than Erik and had red hair too, but it was a nicer red than Erik's, kind of gold-red and silky. If she were a dog, you'd want to pet her all the time. She had green eyes and laughed a lot. She bit her nails, which he was kind of glad about because it meant that she had some hang-ups too. She was crazy about horses and was at Smitty's stable a lot, which was why she was never home when he went there to play chess with Erik.

Angie *did* answer the phone. And he forgot what he was going to say at first. Like he had mashed potatoes in his skull instead of a brain.

"Erik's sick, Horatio," she said. "He's got a super-bad cold."

"We have a big chess tournament Saturday. Do you think he'll be okay by then?"

"He looks awful now. And I think he has a fever."

"What's he doing?"

"Sleeping. He doesn't even feel like reading his chess books. So you know he's got to be sick."

"Well, tell him I called."

"Okay."

"How's your horse doing?"

"Lila isn't really my horse. Smitty's just nice. He never gives her to anyone else to ride when he knows I'm coming."

"Which is every day."

Angie laughed. "I guess. Well, I'll tell Erik you called."

"Thanks."

In the fall while he was out with Silver Chief, he had walked over to Smitty's stables and stayed in the trees so no one could see him. He had spotted Angie. Red hair made her easy to find. She was practicing jumping with Lila. He watched for ten minutes and then cut back through the trees, and she never knew that he had been there.

As he walked home he saw O.P. out for a little air. Even in a down jacket he looked thin as a fence post. Mollie usually trotted alongside him. Now he was alone.

He's got to get another dog, Horatio thought. A little time had to pass, he knew that. There were so many great dogs needing homes. At the shelter in Chicago, Horatio could have taken any one of twenty and been happy. He wished that were true of fathers. He'd walk into this big warehouselike room that had rows of offices with fathers in them. Then he'd walk down the hall and pick out a good dad, one who fit, who looked at him in a way that made Horatio feel he had known him for a long time.

Could there be one more father in the world who wore Peanuts sweatshirts and liked to eat bagels out by the lake and yell lines from King Lear?

He'd tell his mom to talk to O.P. about a new dog when the time was right.

O.P. lifted his gloved hand in a wave. "Warm day, Horatio. I think I can smell spring."

"Yeah, all the snow's gone."

O.P. rested on his cane. "I don't know if I thanked you for your help with Mollie."

Horatio shifted from one foot to the other. "That's okay." *I should walk with him for a while,* he thought. But he just told O.P. that he'd see him at home and began jogging.

He had always taken long walks with his dad. But O.P. wasn't his dad.

He slowed down when he could see his house and walked the rest of the way. Their mailbox had *Tuckerman* and *Berg* written on it. It used to be okay with him that he and his mom had different names, but now with his dad gone, he wished she were a Tuckerman and not a Berg. They would seem more like a family. He guessed he could change his name to Berg. Horatio Berg. Then he could use his initials as a nickname. H.B. No more Hot Turds.

But what could H.B. stand for that would be gross? That was the test. Let's see . . . Hot . . . Buns.

He'd stick to Tuckerman.

7

Horatio saw O.P. waiting in front of the school in the old blue Ford. He stepped out of the flow of kids pushing through the doors of the building and stood against the wall of the entry hall. Pulling his daypack off, he went through the motions of rearranging his books just to gain a few seconds.

Going with O.P. to scatter Mollie's ashes was the last thing in the world he wanted to do.

"I know this brings up a lot of hard memories for you," his mom had said that morning as she left for work. "But I think you can handle it."

How did she know what he could handle? He didn't even know himself.

It was hard to tell how upset O.P. was. He acted pretty normal, asking him how his day had been, driving his usual twenty-five miles an hour. But he could be faking. Horatio knew about that. You get good at it after a while.

When they got to the vet's, Horatio waited in the car

while O.P. went into the building. He came out a moment later carrying a small box. It was just an ordinary box. Anything could have been in it. He placed it carefully on the backseat.

They didn't talk. Horatio watched the snow falling, each flake large enough to be seen separately. They settled on fence posts and mailboxes and nearly covered the sign by the fruit stand that still advertised watermelon and strawberries for sale.

O.P. pulled into the parking spot beside the litter barrel, put on his gloves and opened the car door. "You wait here, Horatio. I know this is hard for you." He opened the back door and removed a metal urn from the box he had placed on the seat. "I'll just walk down the trail a bit."

"I'll follow behind with the flashlight," Horatio said.

O.P. began to walk, using the cane like a blind man, probing the space he was moving into. It was perfectly quiet, as if the day itself was holding its breath.

When O.P. stopped at a small stand of aspens, Horatio was right behind him. The old professor handed him his cane and stood very still for a moment, head bowed. Then he tipped the urn, moving it in a wide arc in front of him. Ashes, fine as dust motes, fell to the ground and were absorbed quickly into the wet earth. O.P. spoke in a low voice.

Rocked in the cradle of the deep,
I lay you down in peace to sleep.

Horatio bowed his head and watched the ashes disap-

44

pear into the earth. O.P.'s voice gathered strength.

Death, a necessary end, will come when it will come.

Snow fell gently, making O.P.'s hair glisten and laying epaulettes on the shoulders of his coat. Brushing a snowflake from his cheek, he reached for his cane, stood silent for another moment and then began walking the slushy path back to the car, Horatio lighting the way with the flashlight. Trees, heavy with snow, blocked the darkening sky.

They were almost home when O.P. spoke. "I'm glad you were with me, Horatio."

Horatio nodded. He was feeling sad, but it was a good kind of sadness. He hadn't known that sadness could feel okay. Seeing the ashes hadn't bothered him the way it had at the campfire with Uncle Stewart. Mollie was part of the earth now, and out of the earth grew the aspens that had gathered around him and O.P. like old friends.

"Grandpa, what you said about death coming when it will come. I suppose that was Shakespeare."

"Brutus spoke those words at Caesar's burial."

O.P. steered the car to the far right to let a speeding pickup truck roar by.

"Wow!" Horatio said. "He must be going ninety."

O.P. smiled wryly. "Hurried and worried until we're buried and there's no curtain call. Life's a funny proposition, after all."

"That's not Shakespeare."

"No, that's from a song by George M. Cohan. Joshua used to sing it. He liked Cohan's music."

"Yeah, now I remember. Sometimes he'd sing that in the shower."

"It's a good shower song. Do you ever sing in the shower, Horatio?"

"Sometimes."

"What do you sing?"

"Oh, anything that comes into my head."

"The world is composed of two kinds of people, those who sing in the shower and those who don't. I'm glad to know you're a shower singer."

"Are you?" Horatio couldn't imagine O.P. singing in the shower.

"I was. But now I must concentrate on keeping my balance." He glanced at Horatio. "Cohan was right, Horatio. Life is a funny proposition. You'll see the truth of that as you get older."

"I'm old enough now."

O.P. didn't say anything. But when they got out of the car, he put his arm around Horatio in a quick hug before they walked into the house.

8

hursday, and Erik still hadn't returned to school. Horatio decided to stop off at his house and see how he was doing.

Angie answered the back door. She was barefoot and her hair was in a fat braid, which made her look different. More of her face showed.

"Erik's at the doctor's," she said.

"Do you know when he'll be back?"

"He just went with my mom about five minutes ago." She shivered. "I'm freezing." She went back inside the kitchen, leaving the door open, which Horatio decided to take as an invitation to follow.

"Erik's cold's turned into laryngitis," she said. "He can hardly talk."

"He won't be at the chess tournament, then?" What a stupid thing to ask!

"No. He's mad about that. Oh, if I burnt them!" Angie grabbed a hot pad, opened the oven door and pulled out a pan of cookies. "I guess they're okay. Open the door, please!" She rushed past him out to the stoop and put the pan down in the snow.

"They'll cool out here faster." She walked back in, slamming the door behind her.

"What kind of cookies?"

"They're my invention. I put in chocolate chips, raisins and nuts for Erik, and butterscotch chips and marshmallows for me."

"Sounds . . . great."

"Want to try one?"

Angie retrieved the cookies from the stoop. One slid off the pan into the snow.

"I can eat that one," Horatio said.

"Leave it for the birds." She slid a spatula deftly under a cookie and handed it to him. "Here. Aren't you dying of the heat with that jacket on?"

Was she inviting him to take it off and stay? He just stood there with the cookie. Like a nerd. He'd better take a bite. He hoped they weren't gross tasting.

"Hmmm. They're good."

"You sound surprised."

He unzipped his jacket. But Angie didn't tell him to take it off. "They're more like candy than cookies."

"Yeah, my mom says too many of them'll rot my teeth. Hey, guess what? My mom's dentist was sick so she had a checkup with your mom yesterday."

"I hope she doesn't have eroding gums."

Angie screwed up her face. "What's that?"

"Soil erodes, trees fall out; gums erode, teeth fall out."

Angie laughed. "What do you do if you have eroding gums?"

"You floss. Every day. Even if you hate it, which I do. My mom has a pottery workshop in our basement, and she made this giant molar and painted 'Floss!' on it and hung it in the bathroom. I keep banging my head on it."

"I'd still rather have a mom who's a dentist than one who does what mine does."

"Your mom writes cookbooks, doesn't she?"

"Yeah. Now she's doing a series called 'The Adventurer's Guide to Healthy Eating.' In the last book the adventures were with different kinds of beans. This one's with tofu."

"My mom buys tofu and never eats it. It just sits in the refrigerator in that slimy water."

"She might want this book, then. My mom tests all the recipes on me and Erik so she'll be sure they won't kill anyone."

"Do you like tofu?"

"No! I make up poems about how awful it is and paste them on the bathroom mirror. It hasn't helped." Angie looked at the ceiling as if one of the poems were written there and began to recite:

> *Tofu is awful,*
> *A terrible jawful,*
> *It should be unlawful*
> *To feed it to your kid.*
> *I nearly died when my mom did.*

Horatio smiled. "I bet my grandfather could come up with a quote from Shakespeare about tofu. He's got a Shakespeare quote for everything."

"They didn't have tofu when Shakespeare lived!"

"Hey . . . wait. I've got one!" Horatio could hardly keep the triumph out of his voice. "Tofu or not tofu. *That* is the question."

Angie giggled. "Hey, can I use that? My mom will be really impressed."

"Now you've got to come up with something on flossing."

"Hmmm . . . Let's see, what rhymes with floss? Gloss, boss, sauce, moss . . . hmm . . . moss . . . If you don't want your teeth growing moss, you'd better start now"—Angie raised her fist—"and FLOSS, FLOSS, FLOSS!"

Horatio laughed. "I guess plaque *is* a little like moss."

"Maybe. Anyhow, take another cookie. And I've got to get going. I've got a clarinet lesson."

Horatio pulled a chess book out of his daypack. "Could you give Erik this?"

"Okay. Any messages?"

"Tell him I hope he gets his voice back soon. And thanks for the cookies." He took a bite of the second cookie Angie handed him and was out of the house, down the steps and a block away before he started running.

He had just hung out with Angie! And it hadn't been a total disaster. His daypack bounced against his back like a big hand slapping him "Congratulations!"

He stopped running. Suddenly he didn't feel so good. Those cookies were heavy. They had fallen like lead to the bottom of his stomach and were just sitting there.

Oh well, he thought. Tofu or not tofu.

He started running again.

9

It was Saturday, nearly a whole week since Mollie had disappeared. Last Saturday it had been too cold to ice skate and today it was too warm and the ice was no good. Anyhow, Horatio didn't feel like being out on the ice. It might start him thinking about Mollie's death. It came up in his mind too much already.

When it did, he tried to block it off by thinking about something really great. Sometimes he couldn't come up with anything, but today he had hanging out in Angie's kitchen to replay over and over again.

When the phone rang, he was sure it was his mom or one of her friends. Maybe Pink Gums Paul. He'd tell him she joined Dentists in Space and just took off for Mars.

It wasn't Pink Gums. Definitely not. It was Angie!

"Horatio, I'm calling for Erik. He's going bananas. He asked me to bring some chess problems over to you that he's been working on. And then you can call and tell him what you've figured out. He's still not supposed to talk much."

"Okay. I'll be around." (Cool. He was so cool.)

"I'm going to the stable now, so I'll drop them off on my way."

By the time the doorbell rang Horatio had changed out of a mud-colored sweatshirt into a blue fisherman's sweater that still had some shape left. He debated whether to change into cleaner jeans, but decided not to go overboard.

Angie was wearing a yellow poncho and high black boots. Her hair was pushed up into a yellow rain hat.

"I didn't know it was raining out," Horatio said.

"It was, but it stopped." Angie pulled off the hat and her hair tumbled out. She handed Horatio an envelope and a book. "Here's the chess stuff."

"I was wondering if you'd like to meet Silver Chief."

"I would. Erik talks a lot about him. He's wanted a dog forever, but my mom's allergic."

When they walked out into the yard, Silver Chief ran to greet them. Horatio rubbed him behind his ears and he flipped over and turned his belly up.

Angie laughed. "Hey, I thought he was a wilderness dog. He's more like a big kitten."

In an instant Silver Chief was back on his feet. He stared at Angie for a second and then took off, running at full speed, ears back, nose into the wind, circling the yard as if he were racing another dog and was determined to win.

"You insulted him," Horatio said. "He's showing you he's no kitten. He could run the Iditarod."

"Silver Chief, I didn't mean to insult you!" Angie yelled.

They watched until Silver Chief had run himself out. Horatio called him, and as he came close Angie managed to land a pat on his head. As if bored with the whole thing, the husky walked away and started chewing at a low-hanging willow branch.

"He's a beautiful dog," Angie said as they walked back to the house. "And I bet he's easy to take care of, too. Easier than a horse. Right now I've got to go and change Lila's straw. It's really grungy."

"I don't know anything about horses."

"Do you want to come and meet Lila? She loves people."

"Yeah, sure." (Cool, was he cool!)

They walked along the lakeshore for a while. The melting snow made the sand soggy. It was easier going when they cut through a meadow. Horatio's foot caught in a deep hole and he pitched forward onto his knees. He got up quickly, embarrassed.

"Are you okay?" Angie asked.

He nodded and followed her through an opening in a barbed-wire fence.

The gate to Smitty's Good Luck Stable had two horseshoes nailed on it.

"A horseshoe's supposed to bring good luck, isn't it?" Horatio asked.

"But you have to mount it with the opening facing up to catch the good luck."

Horatio pushed the gate open and they puddle-jumped to dry land.

"Hi, Smitty," Angie said as a man on a handsome black horse rode up to them. "This is Horatio. Horatio, Smitty."

Smitty smiled, revealing teeth that were stained brown. He smokes, Horatio thought. Smitty was the skinniest man he had ever seen. His cowboy hat came down over his eyebrows and his eyes were black as ink blots. Horatio wondered if he were part Indian.

"Pretty damp around here," Smitty said. "Not a good day for the trails, Angie. You'll be kicking up a lot of mud."

"I came to change Lila's straw."

"There's plenty in the barn. You know where the old stuff goes."

Smitty rode off, and Horatio and Angie jumped puddles to get to a small barn. It was dim inside, and it took Horatio a moment before his eyes adjusted. Three horses swung their heads to look at them. Angie went up to the white one and put her face against its muzzle.

"This is Lila," she said. "And Lila, this is Horatio."

Horatio held out his hand, palm up, the way he had learned to do with dogs. Lila had big, dreamy eyes framed by bristly eyelashes.

"She's beautiful," he said. "What kind of horse is she?"

"Arabian. They're really strong. They have one less vertebra than other horses. That makes their back shorter so they can walk across a desert carrying really heavy loads without getting tired." She nuzzled her face against Lila's. "Hey, I'm changing your sheets today."

"Do Arabians come in different colors?" It sounded as if he were asking about ice cream flavors! What a nerd!

"Sure. Chestnut, black. Lila was born gray. As she grows older she'll get whiter and whiter until she's all white. Now she's in between, with white and gray mixed. You call that dappled."

"You mean Arabians are never born white?"

"Right."

"She's got such gentle eyes."

"I just sit in the barn with her sometimes. She knows when I need some T.L.C."

"What's T.L.C.?"

"Tender loving care."

"I thought it might mean twenty little cookies."

"I don't believe you!" Angie smiled, and Horatio noticed the beginning of a dimple in one of her cheeks. She and Erik really looked pretty much alike. It felt strange and nice both.

"I'll put Lila in a different stall so I can start."

"I'll help," Horatio offered.

The sky had lightened and pale rays came through the one small window in Lila's stall. The straw had a thick smell, almost like dried seaweed. It was heavy, and the rake wasn't that strong. He'd rather lift the stuff out by the handful. He would have if it weren't so . . . what was Angie's word? Grungy.

Angie returned, dragging two large trash barrels. She started raking and they didn't say much, but it felt okay. It actually felt pretty good. He was a little wired, though. Being alone with Angie in this small, cozy place. He knew what some of the guys in school would say if they saw him now. Something dirty that they'd think was cool. Big talkers. Put one of them here with Angie and see what they'd do.

All he knew was that he was feeling good. Angie's hair was the brightest thing in the whole barn. She raked fast, humming. He couldn't figure out the song. Should he ask her?

"What's that song you're humming?"

"Was I humming? Probably 'Four Strong Winds.' It's a folk song."

"I don't know anything about folk music."

"What do you know? Rock?"

"Yeah, and some old songs my dad used to sing."

Angie looked at him, her eyes sympathetic. He turned away, scooped up a pile of straw and dumped it in a barrel.

"You must miss him."

"Yeah."

She had a piece of straw sticking in the bottom of her braid. He reached over and pulled it out.

"Straw," he said, and handed it to her.

Stupid, stupid. They're in the stuff up to their eyeballs and he tells her it's straw!

"Do you ever talk to Silver Chief the way I talk to Lila? Like he's your best friend?"

"Yeah. But he's probably not as good a listener as Lila. He's got to be in the mood."

"Girls are better listeners than boys."

"Better talkers, too."

"They're better inside talkers and boys are better outside talkers. You know what I mean?"

"No."

"Well, girls talk about what's going on inside them, their feelings about things. And boys talk about what's going on outside them, like baseball games, chess tournaments, space stuff." Angie paused as she pushed the dirty straw down into one of the barrels. "My mom's always talking about relating—that's her big word—me relating to Erik and Erik relating to me and me relating to my father. And my dad talks about toxic waste and computers and how much he hates tube socks."

Horatio laughed. "But your dad hating tube socks is real inside stuff. I feel the same way. You always end up with too much sock at the toe and it bunches up inside your shoe and drives you nuts."

"Your dad was a writer, wasn't he?"

"Yeah. Plays."

"I bet you take after him."

"I don't know . . . maybe. Why do you think that?"

"Oh, it's just a feeling. You don't mind that I said that, do you?"

"No."

"I take after my dad in only two ways. I have hair like his and I can crack the knuckles in each of my fingers anytime I want."

58

Horatio winced. "Don't show me."

"Do you want to be a writer?"

"No."

"I think I might. Not cookbooks, though. Travel books. I want to travel all over the world and then write about it."

"Sounds good."

"What do you want to be?" Angie stopped raking and looked at him.

She was waiting. She was probably a super listener. But he had never told anyone what he dreamed of doing. It was his secret. It would get spoiled if he talked about it. He could see it now, his mom bringing him piles of books from the library to read about it. And she and O.P. discussing it at the dinner table, asking him questions, wanting to encourage him. Which is what parents and grandparents are supposed to do, right? Then the secret would be theirs too, not all his.

Angie was waiting. He took the leap, feeling a small tearing as he did it. A letting loose.

"I want to travel and photograph animals—help protect endangered species."

Angie liked that. He could see her eyes warm up. She smiled. "Horatio, I hope you do it. You will. You're smart enough."

He shrugged. And then the pleasure in seeing her response gave way to fear. "Don't tell anybody else what I told you, okay?"

"I won't. But haven't you told Erik?"

He shook his head.

"You've never told anyone about it at all? Your mom?"

"Nope."

"Oh." Angie's eyes grew even warmer. "So I'm the first one you've told."

"You and Lila."

Angie laughed. "You can count on her to keep a secret. She knows a lot of them."

Horatio slowed his raking up. Why go fast and finish? He wanted to make their time in the stable last. "Has your mom ever written anything but cookbooks?"

"Maybe, when she was younger. All I know about are the cookbooks." Angie pushed the last rakeful of straw into a barrel. "Horatio, I worry a lot about my mom smoking."

"Have you told her that?"

"A million times. So has Erik. She smokes the most when she's writing. That's what's so bad."

"My dad too. He finally went to a hypnotist."

"And that worked?"

"Yeah, but he had already smoked for twenty years."

"My dad has tried to get my mom to stop. He tells her it's crazy, she's writing all these books about healthy eating and she's poisoning herself."

"He's right."

"Is smoking bad for your teeth?"

"Smoking is bad for everything."

"If my mom has another appointment with your mom, maybe she could tell her she'd better stop smoking."

"I can ask my mom if she could tell your mom something scary."

"Would you?"

"Sure."

Angie scooped up the last of the old straw and they both pulled the barrels out to the back of the barn, then dragged a bale of clean hay into Lila's stall and began scattering it with pitchforks.

When they had used up all the straw, Angie brought Lila back. "I'd like to groom her. Do you mind if we stay a little longer?"

"No. Can I do something?"

"Just take that curry brush on the shelf there and brush her, hard; but not too hard."

"Does she like it?"

"She even likes when I brush her bangs. Don't you, Lila?" Angie brushed the snowy white hair falling over Lila's forehead. "If she could, she'd purr."

"I bet you spend more time on her hair than on your own," Horatio said.

"Does my hair look that bad?"

"I didn't mean it like that! Your hair is pretty." His face was on fire. He was going to burn up the barn.

Angie blushed and became very intent on taking a tangle out of Lila's mane. "Kids at school say all I think about is horses. But that's because they don't have anything that's special to them. If they did, they'd understand."

"It's like that with me and chess."

"You're lucky. You have two special things, Silver Chief and chess."

As Horatio moved to Lila's other side his hand grazed

Angie's hair. She had a smudge of dirt on her cheek. He wanted to reach over and rub it off.

"You've got dirt on your cheek," he said, his voice a little gruff. She didn't seem to hear him. "Anyhow, I have three and a half special things, not two. The third is being outdoors, seeing wildlife, stuff like that. And the half is photography. When I get the camera I want, it'll get to be a whole instead of a half."

Angie's braid had come loose and her hair was falling over one eye. She pushed it away. "The other day I saw a fox for the first time. It just walked across the trail, looked at me and kept going. I felt so . . . oh, I don't know. Animals, when they look at you and trust you, it's such a good feeling."

"Yeah. That happened to me with a raccoon once."

"I always wonder how photographers get those incredible closeups of animals, like they're just a foot away from this tiger that's ready to pounce."

"They use really strong lenses."

"But still, they've got to be pretty close!"

"Photographing wild animals can be dangerous."

"Does that scare you?"

"No. Not now, anyway."

"Lila's not exactly endangered, but maybe you can practice on her when you get your new camera. I'd love to have a good photograph of her jumping. I want to enter a competition when she's ready."

"Do you have to practice a lot?"

"A lot."

"Erik told me that you helped out at the animal shelter last summer."

"I'm going to do it this summer too."

"I want to get my grandpa to go there. Maybe he'll see a dog he likes."

"Some people don't want to get a new pet when their old one dies. They think the new one will never be as wonderful as the one they had."

"Yeah," Horatio struggled to find the right words. "But a new dog wouldn't have to be like Mollie. It would just be itself . . . you know, great in its own way."

"Have you told your grandpa that?"

"Kind of. Listen, if I get him to go to the shelter with me, would you come too?"

"Sure, if you want me to. It really made me sad when I heard about Mollie. I thought about it all day."

"I wish I could stop thinking about it."

"I know. Well, we'd better get going." Angie planted a kiss on Lila's forehead. "That's your beauty treatment for today."

Horatio stroked Lila's nose. "Good-bye, Lila."

As they walked out of the barn a frigid wind slapped them, swirling a mist of fine snow in their faces.

"It's freezing!" Angie wrapped her scarf around her head.

Horatio pulled on the hat his mom had knit for him with a brim he could yank down over his forehead. He didn't, though. He looked like such a nerd that way.

They didn't talk as they half ran the mile to the intersection. They stopped when they got there. They each had to go in a different direction.

Angie's cheeks looked bright pink above her purple scarf. Snow made her eyelashes shine.

"Just let me know when you want to go to the shelter. And good luck!" She waved, and Horatio watched her run into a world of wind, swirling snow and gray clouds.

10

is mom was in the kitchen. She was wearing jeans and her hair was tied back with a ribbon. Music was playing on the stereo.

"Mozart?" he asked. He was pretty safe with that one. She was always playing Mozart.

"His clarinet concerto."

"You like the clarinet?"

"I never used to, but I do now. I love this concerto."

"Is the clarinet hard to play?"

"I would guess so. Getting your tongue and lips to do the right thing."

He almost told her that Angie was taking clarinet lessons, but he resisted just in time. He motioned to the chopping block filled with fresh vegetables. "Making a stir-fry?"

"A casserole. I saw the recipe in the newspaper."

"Could you put that crunchy crust on it?"

"You liked it? It's just cornflakes and butter." She slit a zucchini expertly down the middle. "Where have you been?"

"I went with Angie to clean out her horse's stall. She needed some help."

"Angie has her own horse?"

"Well, kind of. It's really the stable owner's, but she takes care of her and rides her all the time."

"How's Erik?"

"He's still not supposed to talk."

"Have you found a replacement for him for the tournament tonight?"

"Buddy Burmeister."

"You're probably not happy about that. Horatio, I'm going out with Paul tonight. We made last-minute plans to go to a concert."

"You're supposed to drive me to the tournament!"

"O.P. will drive you. Then he can stay and watch. It'll be a diversion for him."

"I don't want to have to worry about anyone when I'm playing chess!"

"It's such a good chance for him to get out of the house and get his mind off Mollie."

"A good chance for him! What about me?" His voice rose. "You never ask me what I want!"

"Horatio! Shhh!"

"He can't hear. His door's closed."

"I can drive you to the tournament, but we'd have to leave this minute."

"Forget it." He stalked out of the kitchen into his room and flopped on his bed.

That's what he meant about kids having no rights!

■ ■ ■

The front doorbell rang. Pink Gums Paul. He wasn't going to be polite and say hello the way his mom would like him to. He heard her laugh. And then he heard O.P.'s voice. O.P. had come out of his room. He was always polite. Maybe when you were old, being polite when you didn't want to be didn't grind you up inside.

"Horatio."

His mom stood at the door of his room. She had her green eyelids on.

"I'm going, Horatio. I'm sorry about tonight. We'll have a good talk tomorrow. Do you have some time?"

"For what?"

"For a talk. Maybe we can go out for Sunday breakfast."

"Maybe."

"Good luck tonight. I hope Buddy does brilliantly."

"Thanks."

And she was gone. He could smell that rose perfume she wore. And then it was gone too. The front door slammed, and a car motor started. Wheels scrunched on the gravel driveway. Pink Gums had a pretty dumpy car. Sounded like he needed a new muffler.

O.P. wanted to get going pretty early, which was all right with Horatio.

"It's nice to see Evie go out and have a good time," O.P. said as they drove down the empty street.

Horatio didn't answer.

"Is it hard for you to see your mother go out with a man, Horatio?"

He hadn't asked for this! He was supposed to be staying calm, getting his chess head screwed on. "Grandpa, I can't talk about this now, okay?"

"Of course, Horatio. You have a serious evening ahead of you."

That was the end of the conversation. O.P. drove without saying another word, and Horatio closed his eyes and tried to clear his mind. Fat chance!

When they pulled up to the community center, O.P. didn't get out of the car.

"Good luck, Horatio."

"I thought you were coming in."

"No, you go ahead. Call when you're ready to be picked up."

"But Mom said you were going to stay."

"Evie worries about me too much. Play well."

Horatio got out of the car, and O.P. waved and drove away.

The custodian of Spring Creek Community Center was a broad-shouldered, cheerful man who communicated by smiling and winking. He was setting up tables in the meeting room. The center had just been redecorated, and the newly varnished floors were polished to a hard shine. The ugly mustard walls were now white, a welcome change. If only they hadn't rehung those awful photographs of all the dead park presidents, Horatio thought. He was sure by their expressions that they all had had trouble with false teeth. None of them were smiling.

He set up his chess set on one of the tables and sat down. Then Buddy walked in. He looked pretty hyper.

"Hi, Horatio." Buddy pulled off a red tasseled hat, letting loose a springy mass of blond hair. He had very pale skin and sharply cut features, like a Pinocchio puppet. "I thought I'd be the first one. My dad dropped me off. He wanted to watch, but he makes me nervous. What's wrong with Erik?"

"Laryngitis."

"Oh, he'll be sick for a while, then. I'll fill in for him next Saturday too."

"He might be back."

"No way!" Buddy exclaimed.

When Pete and Jerry walked in, Pete looked at Horatio. "My head isn't screwed on straight tonight. I hope yours is."

"Mine's mashed potatoes," Horatio said.

The guys from the competing team arrived a minute later, followed by Rudy, the tournament director. He had on a flowered yellow tie and green plaid pants.

"Rudy, where did you get that clown suit?" Buddy slapped him on the back.

"All right, gentlemen, set up your boards," Rudy said.

And the chess evening was officially under way.

11

There was a knock on his door. His mom. She was home early.

"Come in," he said.

The minute he saw her, he knew something was wrong. Her eyes looked as if she had been crying. She had put on an old wool shirt over her dress and she was holding it around her as if she were freezing.

"How did the chess match go?" She sat down at the foot of his bed, barely missing his toes. "Sorry! We'll have to buy you a king-size bed soon!"

"We lost. It was my fault. I dropped a knight. I couldn't concentrate."

"Oh." She pulled a Kleenex out of the shirt pocket and wiped her nose. "Do you feel awful?"

"Yeah."

"That's why you're not sleeping yet?"

Horatio shrugged. He pulled himself up and sat against the pillows. "I guess."

"Why couldn't you concentrate, Horatio?"

"I don't know."

She was going to try to get him to talk. Pull him into one of those discussions that wore him out. He just wanted to disappear into a hole. No, what he'd really like was to see Angie and Lila. Horses were so peaceful. We ought to learn from them, he thought. We should shut up for maybe a year, just walk and look at the trees and maybe the whole world would straighten out.

"Horatio, I lost my match too." She smiled ruefully. "I got creamed."

What was she saying? He looked at her, waiting for her to say more. But she didn't. She just sat there, wiping her nose.

"How did you get creamed?"

"Well, I know Paul isn't your favorite person in the world, but then, no man I went out with would be, would he?"

Horatio felt his gut tighten. Here it goes. No matter how hard he tried to stay out of it with her, she oozed him in.

He pulled his blankets up. "I miss Dad."

She looked away from him, down at her hands, rubbing the spot on her finger where her wedding band used to be. "I wake up and turn over and expect to see him in bed next to me. And when he's not there, I feel like he's just behind a screen and if I could tear the screen away, I'd be able to touch him."

"But Mom, how—Oh, I don't know . . ."

"What don't you know?"

"Forget it."

"No, tell me what's bothering you."

"If you still miss Dad so much, how can you go out with some other man?"

Evie wadded the Kleenex and stuffed it in her pocket. "You always have asked hard questions, Horatio."

"But Mom, how can you have a new guy come to the house and go out somewhere, and then doesn't he want to kiss you and stuff? I mean, I don't understand. If I were you, I couldn't do it."

Evie smiled. "You couldn't, huh? Well, I understand how you feel. But Horatio, I didn't go out with a guy, meaning Paul, until a year and a half had gone by without your father. That's a pretty long time to be lonely. So I said to myself, well, are you going to close up shop and live on memories, or are you going to do what might hurt? Take a chance and go out with a guy and maybe have a terrible time, but maybe it will be all right. Maybe you'll even enjoy yourself. So I decided to try."

She picked up one of Horatio's shirts from the floor and wiped her eyes. "So, I went out with Paul and got to like him and thought maybe this might not be forever, but for now, it feels good. He made me want Saturday nights to come again. But I got creamed, Horatio. The woman he had been going with for five years when he lived in Indiana has changed her mind about living here. She's coming. And"—she rolled the shirt into a ball and threw it across the room—"I'm going."

Horatio climbed out from under the blanket and patted her awkwardly on the back. "Mom, I didn't want you to get creamed."

"I know that, Horatio."

"Can I ask you something?"

"Just make it easy."

"Doesn't it freak you out to eat dinner with someone who has gums that are eroding away?"

Evie laughed and hugged him. He hugged her back, and they hung on to each other and didn't let go.

She was the first to break away. "Let me straighten your bed, Horatio."

Horatio stepped down on the floor and Evie fluffed the pillows, smoothed the sheet and then held the blanket back.

He climbed in and she tucked the blanket close around his chin and under his feet the way he used to like it when he was little.

"Good night, Horatio."

"Mom, we've got to get Grandpa to the animal shelter. Maybe he'll find a dog he likes."

"Perhaps he'll be ready to think about it after more time passes."

"But it's like part of him is missing . . . you know what I mean?"

"Yes . . . I know what you mean. Now you better settle down and get some sleep."

"Mom."

"Yes?"

"I don't think you lost the match. Pink Gums did. He's the big loser."

She bent down and kissed him good night. It felt like she hadn't done that for years and years.

12

The sun had just hit the edge of his window, laying a bar of light along the floor. It was early enough to spot a deer feeding in the woods if he'd get up and out. What was going on in his mind wasn't all that great that he wanted to lie in bed anyhow.

He heard sounds coming from his mom's studio, right below his room. She was having trouble with the door of her big kiln. He wished he could fix it for her. She must not have slept very well to be working this early.

He stretched, rolled out of bed and picked up the clothes he had discarded on the floor. He'd better do his laundry. He was at the point where there were more clothes on the floor than in his drawers. He was the only kid he knew who had to do his own laundry. His dad's influence. He had always shared housework with Evie and saw no reason why Horatio couldn't throw his own dirty clothes into the washing machine. Although it was a drag, Horatio hadn't been able to find a reason why his father wasn't right.

He put on clean clothes except for his jeans and dumped two armfuls of dirty clothes down the chute. He'd get to the laundry sometime that day. Not now. And he wasn't up for that early walk either. All the stuff that had happened the night before hung on him like cobwebs. Through the window he could see Silver Chief lying on a bed of new snow. So clean and white. Much easier than changing straw!

The *Spring Creek Enterprise* was on the kitchen table, and he flipped through it until he found the chess column. His mom came into the kitchen, and he said "Hi" without looking up. He didn't want to see that her eyes were red from crying over Pink Gums. It would make him feel too guilty for being glad that nerd was out of their lives.

"Horatio, that chess column must be really fascinating." She touched his hair lightly as she passed him on the way to the sink, filled the coffeepot with water and put it on the stove. Her eyes weren't red, but she looked wiped out.

"I've got an idea about what we can do today," she said. "There are sled races in Hamilton with over forty husky teams racing. How would you like to go?"

"You hated it when we went last year."

"I wasn't dressed warmly enough. This time I'll wear my down jacket and double socks."

"I've got stuff to do. You don't have to take me."

She walked over to him. "Horatio, look at me."

Horatio lifted his eyes to her face. She looked into them for a moment before speaking. "I'm not taking you. We're going together, you and I. Okay?"

Horatio could see his reflection in her eyes. "Okay."

"I'll make breakfast, then finish up some glazing. Can you be ready by nine thirty?"

And then she took the eggs out of the refrigerator and the pecans and flour out of the cabinet, and he knew she was going to make pecan pancakes for breakfast.

13

Should he try to talk to Angie at school about going to the shelter or should he call her at home? He decided to call. Erik was still saving his voice, so he probably wouldn't answer the phone. The chances were good that Angie might.

He lucked out. She did.

"O.P. said he'll go to the animal shelter, but just to look," he told her. "I'm hoping he'll see a dog that he just can't resist, though." He guessed he was nervous because he talked on and on about O.P. finding a dog as if someone had wound him up.

"It's so good O.P. is going, Horatio. I didn't think he would," Angie responded.

"Yeah." Horatio hesitated. "I think he's going because my dad died two years ago today and he's trying to be nice to me."

"Oh, well . . . it's good for him to have something to do too."

"We'll pick you up in front of the library at three fifteen. All right?"

77

"Right. Hey, my mom doesn't have eroding gums. I asked her."

Horatio laughed. "That's good. How's she doing on her tofu book?"

Angie groaned. "Last night she tested tofu-and-spinach pancakes out on us."

"Does your dad have to eat all that weird stuff too?"

"When he's home. But he travels a lot."

"I would too if I were him."

Angie thought that was pretty funny. He did too, actually. When he had hung up the phone, he couldn't think of one totally nerdy thing that he had said. It felt good, not being mad at his nerdy self. It felt so good, he went down to the basement to do his laundry. His mom had said that if he waited one more day, he'd be able to donate his clothes to science for research on molds.

O.P. backed the car out of the driveway. "I'm counting on you for directions, Horatio."

"I told Erik's sister, Angie, that we'd pick her up at the library. She's been there before."

O.P. nodded.

He looks pretty miserable, Horatio thought. Maybe I shouldn't have pushed him into going to the shelter.

O.P. drove slowly, his hands gripping the wheel. He was wearing the new green-and-blue-striped scarf that Evie had given him. She had said it was time for him to wear something that wasn't brown or gray. But his jacket was brown. And his pants. And his shoes.

As they pulled up in front of the library, Angie dashed

out. "I had to wait for a science book forever!" She scrambled into the backseat.

"Angie, this is my grandpa. Grandpa, this is Angie."

"It's a pleasure to meet you, Angie," O.P. said.

"I'm glad to meet you, too."

"Horatio tells me you're our navigator."

"Just take this street all the way to County H. Then take a right to Peace Mill Road. About a mile down we'll see the sign for the shelter."

Angie sat back in the seat and Horatio didn't know what to talk about. He'd just be quiet. It didn't seem right to talk about things that would leave O.P. out.

Soon after they turned onto Peace Mill Road they saw the white sign with a green silhouette of a collie on it. They bumped along between overhanging oak trees until they came to the shelter, a sprawling blue farmhouse with a maze of kennels and dog runs along the rear. A small boy was trying to coax a brown-and-white puppy into a car.

Angie smiled. "Look how serious that little kid is!"

"Getting a dog is serious business," O.P. said.

As they walked to the office a dog in one of the kennels spotted them and started to bark. It was like a signal. Another dog began barking, then another and another until the whole kennel joined in.

O.P. covered one ear with his free hand. "Quite a cacophony!"

"What a funny word," Angie said. "What does it mean?"

"A jumble of loud noises."

"Yeah, and guess what you call a lot of chickens squawking? A cacklephony." Horatio grinned. "My dad figured that one out."

The woman at the desk in the shelter office was short and squat, stuffed into a yellow T-shirt that had PUPPY POWER written across the front with a sprinkle of paw prints. Her eyes, one green and one brown, caught Horatio's attention. Two different-colored eyes were common with huskies. Had she been working with dogs so long that she had begun to look like one?

She had a friendly smile. As soon as she spoke Horatio liked her.

"How can I help you today?"

"With your permission we would like to visit the dogs," O.P. said. "We aren't interested in choosing one today, however."

"That's okay. Just start in that corridor through there and keep going. The far door will lead you to the outside kennels. I'll be glad to answer any questions."

O.P. motioned to Horatio and Angie to go first.

Dogs! So many different sizes, breeds, shapes and color combinations. Most of the dogs were so eager for company that they pressed their faces against the wires, barked, wagged tails, pushed paws through openings, licked any hand that came close enough to reach.

Horatio glanced at O.P. How was he taking this? He couldn't tell. The old man walked slowly, stopping, putting his hand out to touch a wet nose or stroke a paw.

"Look at this sweetie!" Angie was getting her hand licked by a caramel-colored puppy with wistful brown eyes.

"I could never work here," Horatio said. "I couldn't stand seeing these dogs disappointed. People coming by and then walking away and leaving them."

They came to a cage in which a large black dog was sleeping. But as soon as she heard their voices she sat up and looked at them.

Angie put her hand through the wires and the dog walked over. She stroked its head. "She's so gentle. What a sweet face for so big a dog."

"Most likely a senior citizen," O.P. said.

"She seems friendly. Look, she's licking Angie's hand."

"Doesn't she have a nice face?" Angie asked, looking at O.P.

O.P. raised his eyebrows and smiled. "I suspect some campaigning is going on here."

He moved on and stopped at a small kennel in which a medium-size, shorthaired dog was pacing back and forth. She had only three legs.

"She must have been in some kind of accident," Horatio said.

"You've had a time of it, old girl." O.P. put his hand against the cage and the dog barked.

"She has some terrier in her, I bet," Angie said.

"She reminds me of a lion in the zoo the way she paces back and forth."

O.P.'s voice was sympathetic. "She's having a hard time, confined in that small space."

A bark sounded that was so mournful Horatio and Angie looked at each other. They followed the sound to a cage where a black-and-white dog with a pink nose was lying with its face on its paws, letting out an end-of-the-world howl.

Horatio squatted and looked the dog in the eyes. "It's going to be okay, buddy. Someday someone will take you home." The eyes just looked at him, steady and yearning. "Maybe O.P. won't be able to turn this one down, Angie."

But O.P. walked by the sad dog without stopping.

When they had passed through the whole kennel, O.P. went back to the senior citizen's kennel and then the three-legged dog's. But after a couple of seconds he was ready to go.

"I guess it didn't work," Angie whispered to Horatio as they walked behind O.P. on their way to the car. "That black dog would have been perfect!"

"Yeah, that's what we think. But what does he think?"

O.P. didn't tell them what he thought. When they had walked back to the car, he suggested that they all sit in the front seat. Angie sat in the middle, pulled off her hat and rested her head against the back of the seat.

"The woman at the shelter said they might have to put that three-legged dog to sleep," O.P. said.

"Why?" Horatio and Angie demanded at the same time, their voices mirroring their distress.

"The shelter is small, and they're not allowed to keep dogs that someone isn't going to take home."

They turned quiet then. O.P. leaned forward intently. Visibility was always a problem for him at twilight.

Horatio was pressed so close to Angie he felt his skin tingle. The heater warmed his legs and the car tires hummed. They rolled by dark silos and hulking barns and then a farmhouse with windows that glowed. He thought of a warm kitchen and a family sitting around a table at dinnertime eating and talking.

"Tired?" he asked Angie.

"Just sad for some of those dogs. I feel so awful when I see an animal that's hurt or lonely."

In the dim light her face looked . . . what was the word Horatio wanted? Enchanted. Like the long-haired princess in that fairy-tale book O.P. had given him when he was little.

"I saw a fawn once that was hit by a car. It was just lying on the road, and when I looked at it, a big tear rolled down its cheek."

"Oh, Horatio! A tear? Are you sure?"

"Yes, one big tear."

"What happened to the fawn?"

"A farmer called the animal warden, but I had to go before he came for the fawn. I've never stopped thinking about it."

They arrived at Angie's house much too soon. Horatio hated to have her leave the warm, dark cocoon they had been enclosed in. The minute she waved to them from the doorway of her house, he began figuring how he could see her again.

14

The house looked closed and dark by the time Horatio and O.P. pulled in the driveway. Horatio had hoped his mom had come home early. It didn't happen often, but when it did, the house was so much easier to walk into. The other day when her last appointment was canceled she had baked gingerbread, and he smelled it the minute he opened the door. Or if she got home really early, she might be down in her studio working on her pots.

He flicked on the lights, turned the thermostat up and went into the kitchen. O.P. followed. The Old Professor wanted to say something to him, but was having a hard time.

"Should I put up some water for tea, Grandpa?"

"No, thank you." O.P. sat down at the table, opened the newspaper he had left there that morning, then folded it again. "This is a hard day, Horatio."

"Yes."

"Perhaps it would help to share our feelings with each other."

Horatio was just going to check if there were any leftovers in the refrigerator. It didn't feel right to do that now.

O.P. continued. "I often have the feeling that the order of things has gone awry. The record keeper up there made a mistake and called the wrong Tuckerman. Joshua should be here with you, not your old grandfather."

Horatio walked to the sink. "Want a glass of water, Grandpa?"

"I'm going to light a memorial candle for Joshua now. I'd like you to be with me. Is that all right with you?"

Horatio nodded and followed O.P. into his room. It was hard to believe this space had once been his. Books were on shelves, stacked on the floor, piled on O.P.'s desk. Framed scenes from Shakespeare's plays covered the wall and plants crowded the windowsills. A photograph of his dad and O.P. stood on the table by the bed. They had their arms around each other's shoulders and were smiling. His dad had hung that same photograph on the wall of his study. Pain, as sudden and sharp as a beesting, made Horatio look away from the smiling faces to the candle O.P. was placing on the bookcase. The Old Professor struck a match three times before it ignited, but when he lit the wick, his hand was steady. Fire leaped up, and Horatio stood beside him, watching it burn down to a small, steady, blue-red flame.

The front door opened and Evie's loaded purse thumped to the floor. Two more thumps. She had kicked off her shoes.

"Anybody home?" she called.

"We're in my room, Evie."

Evie walked in and collapsed in the easy chair. "I was hoping to walk in the house and see a new dog." She looked at the burning candle for a moment, then leaned back, her arms hanging loosely. The hood of her jacket had flattened her hair and she had eaten all her lipstick off. "I walked by the lake for a while, but that didn't help."

O.P. took off his glasses, polished them with his handkerchief and put them on again.

"What would you both think of sharing a few moments of remembrance together? Perhaps we could each choose something appropriate to read?"

"Something that Joshua loved," Evie said, vitality returning to her voice. "I'd like that, O.P." She turned to Horatio. "What do you think, Horatio?"

He couldn't answer. He felt as if he had been squeezed into a very small space with no air to breathe.

"You and your father did so much reading together," she continued. "There must be something you could share with us."

He looked at them tensely. "I don't want to read! What good will that do?" He ran to the front closet, yanked his jacket off a hanger and pulled the door open.

"Horatio, wait!" Evie ran after him, but he slammed the door and ran out of the house, down the driveway to the road, his legs pumping, the wind chilling his flaming face. The gravel spurted out from under his feet. Headlights, tiny orbs at first, grew into piercing suns that bore down on him. Dazed, he paused, like an animal that had just run out of the thick woods. He jumped out of the road as the car swerved around him. The driver shouted a curse.

He ran until he couldn't run anymore and stopped under a giant oak and leaned against it, his forehead pressed to its rough bark. Breathing heavily, he grabbed a fallen branch and swung it with all his strength against a tree trunk.

"I want him back!" he shouted. "I want him back!" He swung, hitting the tree over and over until the branch split in his hands. His breath was ragged and his throat ached. He rested against the tree until he was breathing normally again, then picked up an oak leaf, crisp with beginning frost, and held it against his hot cheek.

The moon floated in a gauzy net of clouds. The road, streaked by moonlight, looked dark and deep as a river. He inhaled deeply, and the night air felt as cleansing as the air blowing on a mountaintop. Relief welled up in him. A straitjacket binding his heart had burst. Tears came to his eyes, and he didn't wipe them away. When one trickled into the corner of his mouth, he licked it. Salty as ocean water. Somehow, that comforted him.

When he began walking back home, he moved slowly. Following a new path in his head, he wanted to be sure of its direction. When he reached the house and opened the door, his mom and O.P. were sitting and reading. He looked at them, and they looked at him, but he could say nothing and went to his room.

A knock sounded on his door and when he opened it, O.P. was there, holding a photograph album.

"Horatio, your father put this album together when he was just a couple of years older than you are now. I'd like you to have it." He handed the album to Horatio and walked back to the living room.

Horatio looked at the album with the gold eagle on the cover. Its corners were frayed, and it smelled as if it had been hidden away in a trunk for a long time. Then he sat down on his bed and turned to the flyleaf. Printed on it in white ink were the words *Camp Windstar, 1959. Joshua Tuckerman.* He was surprised to see how closely the printing resembled his own.

The first photograph was a washed-out brown-and-white color and pictured four smiling guys in pajamas in front of a log cabin. The caption said *Doc, Bernie, Abe and Mush.* The next photograph was clearer. A big guy was standing near a lake holding a canoe paddle like a sword. *Mac the Magnificent.* The next photograph— more guys clowning around in the sand. Was that tall, skinny one with the glasses his dad?

He studied the face, then read the caption: *Bernie, Doc, Ray and Yours Truly.* It was his dad. He was smiling and standing with his foot on the chest of a guy sprawled out on the sand.

It felt strange seeing his father as a boy. Strange, and yet good, too, as if he knew him then, that they might have been friends. He wanted to jump into the happy world of those photographs, hang around with those guys, put his arm around his boy-dad.

When he reached the last page, he turned back to the photograph of the boy standing with his foot on his friend's chest. Then he closed the album and put it under his pillow. He would look at it again before he went to sleep.

He could hear his mom and O.P. talking in the living room. He wasn't sure he wanted to be with them, but he didn't want to be alone, either. His mom began to recite:

> *When in disgrace with fortune and men's eyes,*
> *I all alone beweep my outcast state . . .*

His dad had loved that poem. He had recited it the day before he died. He had asked Horatio to sit close to him and he had laid his hand on Horatio's knee as he spoke, his voice surprising Horatio with its strength.

Horatio walked in stocking feet into the living room and stood behind his mom and O.P. They were facing the memorial candle burning on the table in front of the big windows. The moon was clear of clouds now and shone with a clean, bright edge above the aspen branches.

His mom's voice was a little shaky. She stopped, struggled to get a hold of herself, then continued:

> *. . . Haply I think on thee,—and then my state*
> *(Like to the lark at break of day arising*
> *From sullen earth) sings hymns at Heaven's gate:*
> *For thy sweet love remembered, such wealth brings,*
> *That then I scorn to change my state with kings.*

The words hung in the quiet room, shining. After a moment O.P. cleared his throat and spoke very softly. "Evie's recitation was so beautiful that I'll add only a few words:

We are such stuff as dreams are made on
And our little life
Is rounded with a sleep.

His mom moved between him and O.P., took his hand, and then took O.P.'s hand. They stood linked together for a moment before they went into the kitchen to drum up something for dinner.

Horatio stood at O.P.'s open door. The Old Professor was sitting in the tweed chair, reading one of his thick books. He looked up when he heard Horatio's voice.

"Grandpa, do you have one more of those candles that I can burn in my room?"

"No, but take this one."

"Oh, that's all right. Never mind."

O.P. got up and handed him the burning candle. "No, no. I've had it for a while. Now it's yours."

"Thanks, Grandpa."

Horatio returned to his room and placed the candle on the windowsill facing the moon. He felt drained, but quieter, freer, not uptight anymore.

His dad had been such a neat guy. They had done so much together. Sunday afternoon was their special time, while his mom worked in the pottery studio. They loved to go to the Maxwell Street Market and nose around and see what bargains they could find in all the junk and clutter. They'd try on cowboy hats and suede jackets with fringe and laugh at how they looked. Often they'd return with bargains that Evie thought were the ugliest things she'd ever seen, especially the printed ties. One Sunday they made a real find—a ten-speed bike. They bargained for it with an old toothless man with the loudest laugh Horatio had ever heard. He and his dad took turns riding the bike on the bike path in Lincoln Park and then bought food at the deli and had a picnic on the rocks. The wind was so strong it kept blowing their paper plates and napkins away. They didn't want to leave, so they sat in a cave of large boulders and looked out at the whitecaps and the changing colors in the sky.

His dad had just found out that he had lung cancer, but instead of lying around and feeling sorry for himself, he did more than ever, as if he didn't want to miss any chance he could get to be with Horatio and his mom. And he was like that right up to the day he suddenly got worse and had to go to the hospital for the third time and there was nothing anyone could do to keep him from slipping away from them, just as the sun had disappeared that Sunday they had sat on the rocks together. A blazing orange-pink had lit up the whole sky, and then the sun slipped below the horizon and was gone. Horatio had felt cold and had moved closer to his dad, and his dad had put his arm around him and they sat watching the gulls wheel and soar.

Now that he thought about it, he had probably spent more time with his dad in the ten years they were together than a lot of guys spent with their dads in a whole lifetime.

He stretched out on the bed and pulled the blanket up to his chin. The words of the poem replayed in his mind, in his mom's voice, then in his dad's . . . "For thy sweet love remembered, such wealth brings, that then I scorn to change my state with kings. . . ."

He breathed deeply and watched the candle burn below the moon. Even though his father had died young, he wouldn't change places with another kid whose dad might live to a hundred.

Never.

15

fter dinner, the following week, O.P. said he had something he wanted to talk to Evie and Horatio about.

"Let's go into the living room, then," Evie said. "We'll do the dishes later."

"No, Evie, sit down. We can talk here." O.P. waved his hand at her empty chair.

"Horatio, let's just clear the plates. I can't relax at a table full of dirty dishes. Should I put up water for tea?"

"Evie, I don't want to make an event out of this. I simply want to talk to you and Horatio for a few minutes."

"Mom." Horatio picked up her and O.P.'s plates. "The dishes are cleared. O.P. wants you to sit down."

"Well," O.P. said as Evie and Horatio faced him across the cleared table. "As you both know, there has been some talk in this house about my getting a new dog. Horatio particularly has been urging me to go to the shelter again. I didn't want to do that. You see, I had decided not to get a new dog."

"But Grandpa . . ."

O.P. raised his hand. "Just hear me out, Horatio, please."

Horatio sighed and sat back in his chair.

"I've felt that no dog could replace Mollie, but there's also another reason. I am an old man who is alive by the grace of a pacemaker." He smiled at Horatio. "I think, Horatio, I could be classified as endangered."

"O.P., people with pacemakers live years and years," Evie said, distress sharpening her voice. "I know a woman—"

"Evie," O.P. broke in. "I'm taking too long to tell you that I've changed my mind. I may get another dog. But only if I'm sure you both realize that a new dog might outlive me. Evie, but mainly you, Horatio, would then have to care for it."

Horatio met O.P.'s intense eyes. "I've already thought of that, Grandpa."

"Ah, so, Horatio." O.P.'s voice was gentle. "Would you be able to love a dog with only three legs?"

Horatio stared at O.P. as he digested his words. Then he smiled. "Yes, Grandpa." He pushed his chair back and stood up. "Mom, we saw this dog at the shelter. She was pacing back and forth in a tiny kennel. And they might have to put her to sleep because they figure no one's going to want her because she's been in an accident and only has three legs. The shelter lady said the rules are that they can't keep problem dogs that no one wants. They don't have the room."

"Wait a minute," Evie said. "Slow up. You mean this dog has three legs and can still run?"

"Her walking is a little . . . bumpy, but she gets around fine. Right, Grandpa?"

"I called the shelter and talked to the woman in charge," O.P. said. "She explained that the dog is nervous because she's caged and that she's very affectionate when she trusts you. She definitely belonged to someone at some time."

"We think she's part terrier, right, Grandpa? She's kind of a reddish brown color."

"Evie," O.P. said. "What do you say about this? We don't want to push you into anything."

Evie was silent for a moment. She looked at Horatio and then at O.P. "O.P., are you thinking of getting this dog because you're worried that she might be put to sleep?"

O.P. sat back in his chair, pressed his palms together and rested his chin on his fingertips. "I have been worrying about that dog, yes, and yes, I don't want her killed. She's a survivor. She's had to fight to live." He paused, then continued. "The fight almost went out of me when Joshua died. But I'm here, and being alive means choosing to move on, not hanging back in the shadows." He dropped his hands into his lap and turned to Horatio. "That's what Horatio has been trying to help me with. And you too, Evie."

Evie walked over to O.P. and put her arms around him. "I love a three-legged man, why shouldn't I love a three-legged dog?" She unhooked his cane from the back of his chair. "Your third leg is just detachable, that's all."

O.P. took Evie's hand in his and turned to Horatio. "Horatio, you're certain about this dog?"

Horatio didn't say anything. He wasn't sure he could trust his voice. He just nodded yes.

"Do you want to pick up Angie so she can go with us to the shelter?" O.P. asked Horatio.

"She's always at the stable on Saturday. Erik may be able to come, though. He's going back to school next week."

"Call and see. I'll be waiting in the car."

Erik answered the phone. "Hey, Horatio, this bird is ready to fly!"

"O.P.'s decided to get a dog! Can you come to the shelter with us? We're going right now."

"Let me ask my mom. Hang on."

In a moment he was back. "Okay! I'll be ready."

"O.P.'s getting a really neat dog. She's missing a leg, but she gets around fine. There was a chance they might have put her to sleep if someone didn't take her."

"Sounds like something O.P. would do."

"Yeah . . . Okay, we'll be there in five minutes."

Erik was waiting outside his house as they drove up. He looked pale and his hair had grown so long it hung over his ears.

"I think it's great that you're getting a dog, Professor Tuckerman," he said as he settled in the front seat.

"We'll both have to get used to each other."

O.P. drove faster than usual. In the shelter parking lot Horatio noticed that he walked toward the office quickly, hardly leaning on his cane.

"We're glad you're back," said the Puppy Power woman. "It's wonderful that you're taking Sky. I never thought she'd get out of here."

"How did you know her name is Sky?"

"She had no tags on, but it had been raining for a week and the day the policeman brought her in the rain stopped and the sky turned blue. So I named her Sky."

Sky was pacing back and forth in the kennel. When she saw them, she barked and jumped against the wires.

"Today's your lucky day, Sky." The woman clipped a leash onto Sky's collar and handed it to Horatio.

"You and Erik take her to the car, Horatio," O.P. said. "I have to sign the papers."

"She's a beautiful color." Erik bent down and put his hand out to pet Sky, but she backed away.

They walked Sky to the car, and she jumped in as if she had been riding in the old Ford all her life. Horatio hugged her, but she wriggled out of his grasp.

"I don't blame you, Sky," he said. "You don't know me well enough for that stuff yet."

O.P. walked to the car, carrying a ragged blue blanket.

"This is Sky's. They had given it to her to sleep on. I thought she should have something familiar to take with her."

Horatio opened the back window as O.P. started the car and Sky thrust her face out, lifting it to catch the wind as they picked up speed.

"Looks like she's used to riding in a car, Grandpa. She loves the wind."

"Good. I can look forward to having a driving companion. Horatio, how do you think Silver Chief will feel about a new dog in his territory?"

"I don't know."

The first thing Horatio did when they arrived home was to take Sky out to the yard to meet Silver Chief. O.P. and Erik went with him.

Silver Chief ran up to them and Sky stood still. She looked frightened. Silver Chief stared at her, then circled her, sniffing.

"She looks so small compared to Silver Chief," Erik said.

Silver Chief put his paw on Sky's shoulder and Sky barked and ran to the fence, then stood there and barked again as Silver Chief ran up to her. Then both dogs circled each other and as if on command, took off and ran the length of the yard, then reversed, ran back, and stopped and looked each other over again.

Silver Chief put a paw out and grazed Sky's nose. Sky ducked her head and batted her shoulder against Silver Chief. Silver Chief leaped, bumping into Sky, and both dogs went down together, a tangle of paws and tails. Sky righted herself and barked as Silver Chief pressed toward her again.

"I think that's enough for the first meeting," O.P. said. "Why don't you call Silver Chief into the house, Horatio?"

Erik smiled. "Silver Chief thinks she's a big toy."

"Silver Chief, into the house!" Horatio called.

But Silver Chief stood his ground, watching Sky.

Horatio ran to him and tugged his collar. "Let's go."

"Sky, come," O.P. said. "That's a good girl."

Once both dogs were in the house, Sky went over to Silver Chief's bowl of water near the kitchen sink. Silver

Chief growled, ran over to the bowl, pushed Sky aside and started drinking.

"Sky, I'll get you your own bowl," Horatio said. He opened the cabinet under the sink and rummaged around until he pulled out a blue bowl. Mollie had used that bowl a long time ago when she had first come from London. He put it back in the cabinet, found an old camping pot, filled it with water and started to walk toward Sky. Then he stopped and handed the pot to O.P. "You give it to her, Grandpa."

O.P. put the pot down on the floor. "Sky, this is for you."

Sky walked over and before she started to drink, she licked O.P.'s hand.

"She's saying thank you, Grandpa."

"I'm glad you met Sky," O.P. said as they drove Erik home. "And thank you for helping Horatio find Mollie."

At the mention of Mollie they all turned quiet. O.P. broke the silence as they approached Erik's house. "Come over and visit again soon, Erik. I'd like you to get to know Sky as well as you knew Mollie."

"I will, Professor Tuckerman."

Horatio didn't expect Angie to call. But she did, the moment she returned from the stable and Erik told her about Sky.

"I dreamed O.P. would get a dog, Horatio."

"Come on!"

"I did. Honest. Is your grandpa happy?"

"Well . . . I think he's happy, but a little sad, too."

"Yeah, I can see how that would be."

"Listen, you didn't really dream that he'd get a dog, did you?"

"I really did. I didn't know which dog, it was just a dog. But the shelter was in my dream. And so were you."

"Me?"

"Yes."

"What was I doing?"

"Flossing your teeth."

"I don't believe you!"

"The floss was bright red and it unraveled from a huge spool, the kind electrical wire is on."

"And every time I moved to a new tooth, sparks flew out, right?"

Angie laughed. "Hey, I'm taking Lila out on the trail tomorrow. Want to come?"

"I can't."

"Why?"

"I'll be flossing my teeth. I've got this big spool of red floss . . ."

"You have to come. I told Lila that you would."

"Well, what time?"

"Can you meet me at the stable at ten?"

"Okay. See you then."

"We have a new woman in the house, Evie," O.P. said when Evie came home. "Her name is Sky."

Evie dropped her packages and put her hand out. Sky

100

approached cautiously, but when Evie stroked her head she backed away.

"She'll have to get used to us," O.P. said.

"She hasn't let being three-legged stop her."

"She's missing a leg, and I'm dragging one. She'll teach me a few things."

Evie hugged O.P. "Congratulations, O.P. I wish you and Sky many happy years together."

Evie had brought home a large veggie pizza with a dessert of chocolate-fudge–mocha cake. Horatio ate until he was stuffed.

"I'm going to walk off some of this dinner," he said. He put on his jacket and went out the front door so the dogs wouldn't see him.

It was a clear night, bright with stars. The trees were black silhouettes rising on either side of him, taller than they ever looked in the daytime. The moon was white as candle wax. Snow muffled his footsteps.

It felt strange walking without Silver Chief. For a moment he looked back, imagining he heard him. No. Just his own prints marked the snow. He thought of the evening he had followed O.P. into the woods to get Mollie and how O.P.'s footsteps had a circle from the cane punched in the snow next to them.

He had told Angie that O.P. had probably felt happy but sad, too, bringing Sky home. He knew that's how *he* felt. Finding Mollie's old blue bowl had brought the sadness . . . the same with his dad's camp album. It had made him glad to see his dad having so much fun when he was a boy. It was almost as if he were there at camp with him. But then, turning the last page of the album, the sadness had come. He had felt sad, too, hearing his mom recite that Shakespeare poem, but then, thinking about the words of the poem as he was lying in bed, he had realized something about his dad dying young that made him feel lighter inside, not so stone heavy. More . . . peaceful.

The low, mellow hoot of an owl startled him. He stopped and listened. He had seen an owl only once, a small horned owl sitting in a tree. So perfect, with those round yellow eyes staring at him.

He wondered if Angie had ever seen an owl. He'd have to ask her.

He walked slowly until he came to the fork in the road, then turned back and walked more quickly when he saw the lighted windows of his house shining through the trees.

O.P. was sitting with his book on his lap. Silver Chief was in his spot under the table.

"Have a good walk?" O.P. asked.

Horatio nodded. "Where's Sky?" And then he saw her, lying against the window wall, half hidden beneath the drapes, the blue blanket under her outstretched paws.

"She's settling in," O.P. said.

"She feels safe there, I guess."

His mom was writing a letter and eating grapes. She had taken a shower, and her hair was wet. He liked her best this way—at home, in old clothes with no makeup

102

on. He hoped she didn't meet a man to go out with for another year or two. Maybe then he'd be ready.

He didn't want to go to his room. It felt good in here with O.P. and his mom and the two dogs.

"Grandpa," he said. "How about a game of chess?"